"My name's Roen," he stated, "not Malling."

"I know that," Clemmie said quietly, pressing close to him.

"Your tongue knows it, but not your heart," he replied. "One day you're going to be my wife, I told you that. But it will only be when Malling's ghost has been laid, when not even a shadow or an echo or a memory remains!"

Deliberately he stepped away from her. "I've never been a woman's comforter, and I don't intend to begin now. Also I don't plan to play second fiddle. When it comes to my woman, I have to be first, last and in between. It's best that you realize that at once...."

OTHER
Harlequin Romances
by JOYCE DINGWELL

Many of these titles are available at your local bookseller
or through the Harlequin Reader Service.

For a free catalogue listing all available Harlequin Romances,
send your name and address to:

HARLEQUIN READER SERVICE,
M.P.O. Box 707, Niagara Falls, N.Y. 14302
Canadian address: Stratford, Ontario, Canada N5A 6W2

or use coupon at back of book.

CHAPTER ONE

THROUGH the open window, had she cared to peer far enough, Alison Coyle could have glimpsed the Pacific Ocean rolling rhythmically into the golden beaches of southern Queensland, she could have seen the high rises like tall poppies of Surfers Paradise, the shining carpets of foothills that soared to the Coyle home on Mount Banjo, but Alison only looked much closer to their nearest neighbour at newly-opened Summer Heights Estate, a Mr Bruce Malling—obviously comfortably placed, Alison's husband had hinted, to be a partner in such a choice land deal, and, on top of that, to build himself such a substantial home.

Alison's husband had built a fine home on Summer Heights Estate, too, but he was not a partner, and also he was not young like Malling. That second point was what was worrying Alison now. Her older daughter Clemmie was at this moment showing Bruce Malling how to mount a pony ... the sections were almost small farmlet size ... and showing him with her usual artless ardour, refreshing to some perhaps, but scarcely conducive to—— Well, let's face it, Alison muttered to herself, there are precious few eligible men in this exclusive place.

She had confessed this fear some time previously to her husband Daryl; a mother had to think of such things.

Daryl, always bland, never apparently perturbed, had smiled fondly back at her.

'I have no doubts about Amber,' he said.

'But Clementine?'

'Mmm. Clementine.' (A heavy pause, though Alison had fondly categorised the hesitation as thoughtful.)

'I see your point, dear,' Daryl Coyle had agreed at length. 'However, Sykes, the Summer Heights rep, has confided to me that the young bachelor partner in the promotion intends building and living here. If Clementine played her cards right she could finish up very comfortable, no staggering fortune as it appears our Amber is getting herself, but satisfactory enough, and particularly satisfactory, Alison, to *us*. For after all, we can't be saddled with Clementine indefinitely, knowing, as we both do, that with Amber it will be quite the reverse. Yes, Alison, I entirely agree. The girl will be placed.'

Alison Coyle had nodded, not even dreaming of correcting that bare 'girl' to 'Clementine', or 'your elder daughter', or even to 'my older stepdaughter', not hearing a harshness. Instead:

'You always think of something, Daryl,' Alison had praised. 'You're always right.'

But Clemmie, Clemmie's mother rankled now, was *not* right, not with that naïve, unstudied, tomboyish approach, in fact Clementine was all wrong. Rumpled jeans, windblown hair, a not far from adolescent gaucherie that Amber, though three years her sister's junior, would never have displayed. Wrong, wrong, wrong, yet while there was no competition, meaning no *Amber* competition, Clemmie might possibly make it. Some men like the outdoorsy approach.

If it happened, Alison's mind ran on, she and her first child would be near neighbours in this new select place. She felt herself withdraw a little, just a little,

for she would have preferred Amber, and as for
Daryl——

Still, it was Daryl himself who had promised, and
promised very generously for a step-parent really:
'The girl will be placed.' How characteristically
thoughtful of Daryl! How considerate!

Dear farseeing Daryl, Alison went on affection-
ately, she could never say of him that he didn't think
things out, look to their future. When, as Alison Green,
she had put her life into Daryl Coyle's capable hands,
following Amber's birth, and after the drowning
tragedy that had spared small Clementine but taken
her first husband Simon, Alison had known that everything would be well.

Now, eighteen years after, Alison knew it more than
ever. With the money that Simon had left her, Daryl
had built a lucrative business, and it had all finished up
here, a retirement in a really beautiful home on a substantial property overlooking perhaps the finest scenery
in all Australia, everything she wanted, everything she
asked, but nicest of all, to Alison's thinking, nice
people with nice manners, nice incomes and nice
taste.——Oh, you little fool, Clementine ... Alison, still
gazing up the hill, framed her lips ... you've just let
the mount push Mr Manning right over, his immaculate jodhpurs will be grass-stained, and he'll dislike
that, he looks the fastidious type. Yes, you utter idiot,
Amber would never have done that. With Amber there
are never any slip-ups, never any fears, never any——

Yet Amber? No fears?

For through the open door Alison could hear her
husband beginning to pace the study, something he
only did when he was annoyed or concerned or upset.
The mail had arrived earlier, and in it, Alison had

noticed, had been a letter from Amber to her stepfather. She had been pleased about that, she had always
been pleased with the closeness of her husband and
Amber, even though, or so she supposed, it was only
natural when——

She had known Daryl had been pleased, too, and
that had been the reason he had hurried to his office to
read the letter. Now the pacing intimated that the contents did *not* please him. Alison crossed quietly to the
door, then went in.

'Dearest?' she asked.

Daryl Coyle, quite strikingly handsome in his late
fifties, turned to his wife.

'I'm very angry, Alison,' he said.

'Is it Amber? I saw the letter.'

'Yes. The poor sweet, the unhappy baby. That
wretch—that rogue! Why, I could ... yes, I
could——'

'What's the matter, Daryl?' she asked anxiously.

'That Rickaboy Roen! I think that was the absurd
name the child said.'

'Yes, Daryl?'

'It's all off,' he snapped.

'The——?'

'Yes.'

'Oh, dear.' After a moment Alison repeated herself.
'Oh, dear!'

'I'd checked him up, too,' Daryl Coyle said. 'I felt
I'd like to be sure—for Amber. The fellow is positively
rolling. He was just what we would want for her, what
she deserves.'

'Then why did she——'

'She didn't. Amber wouldn't. Never Amber. Am-

ber's clever, she's shrewd, she deliberates, not like——
No, it wouldn't be Amber. Yet the thing is done. It's
finished. You can read for yourself.' He handed his
wife the letter, but she did not take it, she had complete acceptance of his word.

'Then what, Daryl?' she asked instead.

'She must come home, of course. Home, anyway,
for a while, the dear girl.'

'I agree. We'll comfort her, give her our support.
Perhaps she might even——' As if by a magnet Alison
Coyle's eyes sought the window again, this time the
study window, but with as clear a view of the neigh-
bouring property ... and Clemmie and Mr Malling ...
as before.

Daryl Coyle, always in perfect tune with his wife and
her thoughts, followed her glance.

He stood a long enigmatical moment. 'Well, now,'
he said.

Presently he crossed and put his arm around his
wife's shoulder, to which she responded with her hand
in his. It was to this affectionate scene that Clementine
Green, arriving soon afterwards, and accompanied by
their new ... and soiled ... neighbour, was greeted, as
she had frequently been greeted, and Clemmie thought
again, as she always had thought, what a handsome
couple they made, and what a loving one.

Putting me where, she wondered a little hollowly,
and putting the memory of Father, and Alison's first
husband, where as well? Clemmie shook off the little
dismay she always felt at such times and came forward
with the young man she had brought down to the
house.

'Hullo, young lovers,' she greeted breezily, 'this here

is Bruce Malling from up the hill but down now to be duly laundered and repaired. Black Prince told him where he got off.'

'He needn't have told it quite so forcefully,' said Bruce Malling ruefully. He indicated the green grass stains that Alison had anticipated but also a patch on the fawn drill at his knee showing red. Red for blood.

Alison gave a little cry and came busily forward. This was what Clementine should have been doing, Clemmie's mother thought resentfully, fussing over the man, petting him, attending to his injury, not making a joke of a fall. However, she had to admit he did not seem to be minding it all that much; his eyes on Clemmie were brightly amused, and his lips quirked.

Not Daryl, though; he was quiet, estimating.

'Mr Malling.' He came forward and shook the younger man's hand.

'Bruce, please. After all, your daughter called me Bruce even before she whispered to her horse to play that filthy trick.'

'Stepdaughter.' It was said pleasantly, but it was still said.

'Quite,' nodded Bruce Malling easily. 'She doesn't resemble you, nor' ... a charming smile at Alison ... 'you, either. Well, not very much.'

'Her father was dark,' Alison provided.

They all looked at Clemmie now, and she squirmed and grimaced. Everyone laughed at her embarrassment ... but Daryl Coyle's laugh was perfunctory. He had never seen Clementine look quite like this before, he was thinking, pink-cheeked, sparkling-eyed, her windblown hair tossed about her face.

'We're upsetting Clementine,' he said mock-indulgently. He turned back to the young man. 'You'll stop for tea, of course.'

'Only after I've taken off his trews and scrubbed him up,' Clemmie promised, recovered from her embarrassment again, quite enjoying the situation, perhaps because it was a new one for her. Now, with Amber ...

'My dear!' protested Alison in maternal reproof.

'I'll put him in a dressing gown and *then* clean the joddies,' altered Clemmie teasingly, 'they won't take long to dry in this sun, and they're non-iron. Then I'll bathe him, anoint him, still' ... mischievously ... 'in the dressing gown, of course.'

'Will I be able to fit into it?' asked Bruce Malling plaintively before Alison could remonstrate once more. 'I presume you're not offering me Mr Coyle's dressing gown?'

'No, my sister's. She's tall and elegant, not scrappy like I am.'

'You mean petite.' Bruce Malling looked with the same bright amusement again on Clemmie. 'But what's this? You have a sister?'

'Indeed,' came in Daryl Coyle promptly. 'My dear wife brought two precious gems to our marriage— Clementine and Amber. Both the girls have their own digs in Brisbane, but Clementine is out of work just now, so——'

'My firm moved south,' Clemmie endeavoured to come in, 'when Lindsay opens his new surgery in Sydney he'll send for me.'

'Surgery?' Bruce picked it up. 'You never said so before. You're a nurse, then? I would be safe having you bathe my knee?'

'Very safe. But I'm a vet nurse.'

'A vet nurse. Now I know why you were so efficient with Bingo.' He smiled at Clemmie, sharing a memory with her.

Aware, though, of a little tension somewhere in Daryl Coyle, why or what he did not know, Bruce asked at once of the older man: 'And your other daughter, sir? Amber?'

'Another stepdaughter.' The briefest of pauses, the briefest of glances at Alison, so brief there could have been no pause, no exchange. 'Amber is a secretary. Here's her photc.' But Bruce was not attending. He was waiting for Clemmie to run the hot water, to ply him with towels, throw in a robe and give him one minute to hand out his jodhpurs. Only Clemmie did not put it that way. As she tossed in the robe she called: 'Get 'em off!'

'Clementine! Really!' Alison called a reproof again.

But it was no use, and Clemmie's mother saw that at once; the girl was almost dancing. Alison had never seen her like this before. She heard the laughter from the bathroom as Clemmie went in to attend the casualty, the squeal as the hot water touched the raw wound, she heard the silence—one could not hear a silence, but Alison felt she heard this one.

She went back into the study. Daryl was putting the phone down, and his handsome face was a study.

'Did you know,' he said to his wife, 'that Malling was one of the big property estate Mallings? The Melbourne Mallings?'

'No, I didn't, dear.'

'That accounts for him being here. It rather puzzled me that such a young fellow could buy himself a partnership in such an exclusive promotion. But he hasn't bought, of course. It would be his.'

'His?' she queried.

'His family's, thus his. So Clementine would have been more than comfortable, wouldn't she?'

A pause from Alison, then: 'Would have, Daryl?'

A pause from Daryl, then: 'That's what I said, dear.'

'But——'

'Yes, Alison?'

'Oh, nothing, Daryl, nothing at all. I mean—— That is—— Oh, please, Daryl, tell me!'

'I intend to, Alison.' Daryl Coyle cleared his throat, paced up and down the room, then returned to his wife's side.

'I think you've just seen for yourself what a forward little fool Clementine is making of herself,' he began directly.

'Well—yes.'

'Amusing for a moment, perhaps, but——'

'But, Daryl?'

'But only for that moment. Then a distaste, even a disgust, would set in. Finally, because of the girl's forward behaviour, a good chance would be lost. Not just for Clementine herself but for any subsequent sensible girl who happened to present herself, particularly a—*related* girl. You follow me, Alison?'

'Oh, yes.'

'In which case it must be quashed at once.'

'How, Daryl?' Alison asked anxiously.

'It must be stopped. Ask yourself, my dear, can we allow this absurd folly to proceed any longer at—Amber's expense?'

'Amber's?'

'Amber's. For it's sure to happen.' A note of pride. 'It always does.'

'But——' began Alison.

'And actually, beloved, anyone would suit Clementine, any man with a horse, a dog or even four feet of any kind. But Amber——'

'Yes ... yes, I suppose so, and certainly if you say so, dear.'

'I do say so, Alison, believe me.'

'But how?'

'The answer is simple,' he said. 'Amber herself.'

'Amber?'

'Yes.'

'But I hardly think we can do anything, Daryl, or if we should do anything.'

'We'll be doing nothing, little goose. Not really. It won't be through any conniving of ours that Amber will be coming home quite soon. She would have come, anyway, following this sad little letter.' As he said it, Daryl Coyle crossed and took up Amber's photo. Amber was fair, like his own dear Alison, but she had the chiselled, aristocratic features of——

Smiling a little, Daryl Coyle put the photo down.

'Here they come now,' whispered Alison. 'Tea in the library, I think.'

'Well, certainly not on the patio, not with the fellow dressed in that garb.'

'It's Amber's.'

'All the same ...'

'He doesn't seem to mind, though,' Alison pointed out.

'Not at the moment. But when the stupidity sets in ...' Daryl Coyle followed his wife out.

'Bruce feels a fool,' Clemmie was giggling. 'I tell him it's nothing to what he looks.'

She was on top of the world, exuberance itself—cloud nine, they called it, Daryl Coyle thought sourly. To hide his resentment he had to look away. But eventually he had to look back again, and when he did he said what he had to with an almost brutal triumph that he found hard to conceal.

'My dear Clementine,' he told Clemmie and the entire room, 'your sister is coming home.'

He put down the cup that Alison had handed him, sat back and smiled round the small gathering.

'Yes, Amber will soon be back.' He said it in triumph again.

No one pursued the subject, and that was what Daryl Coyle wanted. He was glad now that Bruce Malling had only given Amber's photo a fleeting glance, perhaps not even that. He had it planned, even this early. Amber's entry. He had seen it all so often. People talking together, a little laughter, a little argument, then sudden stunned silence. Amber, of course.

He saw his lovely slender girl with the head like a gold chrysanthemum, with the soft fair skin, the pretty pouting mouth. He saw the tallness and sophistication that put all other women in the shade, especially scrappy ... Malling had been kind and said 'petite' ... girls like——

Alison was busy passing and refilling, no time for any talk on Amber, and Bruce Malling was being polite if a little puzzled. Why should Clemmie's sister returning home be announced in a voice like that? Clementine, Daryl noted with a malice he would not have admitted, was unmistakably upset. Oh, she was doing the usual things, saying the expected words, but she was tense, he could tell it by her whitened knuckle-bones whenever, and it was often, she clenched her hands.

They were talking about the Summer Heights Estate now. Yes, Bruce Malling was saying, his father had bought into it, a third of it as a matter of fact, then handed it to his fourth son. Me, Bruce grinned. All the Malling family of four boys had been similarly treated. Bruce leaned over and took a cake. His father, he went on, had believed there was a need up here for—well——

'Gentlemen's homes,' Daryl came in.

'We really meant homes for people needing space for outdoor activities. Riding' ... a sly look at Clemmie ... 'a putting green, a tennis court, a pool, all that.'

'Of course.'

The talk drifted round Clemmie. She contributed very little, and after her animation only a short while ago it soon became obvious. Bruce noticed it, and grew more puzzled.

'What do *you* think, Clemmie?' he asked at length.

What did she think? Clemmie sat fidgeting nervously and trying not to show it. What she thought was this: it was a darn good job that Amber was already settled, or very near settled, because—— Clemmie did not know what her parents knew yet, so at least she was spared that, but on the other hand she did know her sister Amber. Amber was very like the North Queensland crocodile ... Clemmie had considerable knowledge of wild life, she often moaned that it was all she did have ... the Johnson River specimen who attacked only to taste, never to consume. Amber might not want to consume Bruce when she met him, but she certainly would taste, and, the same as with the croc, for the tasted the result could be just as fatal.

'Clemmie, I've spoken to you twice.' It was Bruce, and in laughter. 'Where are you?'

'Drinking tea, like you are, but very near the process of seeing you out.'

'Clementine!' It was Alison once more.

'His trews have dried. I can see the shape on the line. I'll bring them in before they stiffen and he has to alter his outline to them, not them to him.'

She was gone before they could comment, but once away from the library Clemmie did not go straight to the trousers on the line. Instead she put her head against a door and said to the panel: 'No, not Amber. Not now. Some time, of course, because it has to be, but only after—well, after—— No, no, *no*!'

Presently she controlled herself and finished her task.

Bruce retired to the bathroom again and changed out of the robe. When he emerged he handed over the dressing down, saying: 'She must be as tall as I am; also have very good taste.'

'Yes to both,' smiled Clemmie.

'Are you really throwing me out, Clemmie?'

'I am. I—I have to go into Brisbane.'

'Now? Isn't it rather late?' he queried.

'It isn't all that far, and I like evening travel.'

'What an odd girl, you never said this before.'

'About liking evening travel?'

'About going into Brisbane. If you had, I would have come, too.'

'Then come.' Clemmie actually said it, outwardly carelessly but really with an almost fierce intent in her heart. Why not? Why not involve him? Compromise him? It was the only way you'd ever win a male with Amber about. Yet no, it was not, and never could be, her way.

'I can't,' Bruce was saying regretfully. 'I'm expecting an interstate call.'

'Business?' she asked.

'Yes. I hope' . . . mock-serious but still with an intentional note . . . 'yours is.'

'I have to pick up a letter at my flat.' She did not have to, and there probably was no letter there, but the excuse had to suffice. She had to get away for a while, away from her stepfather. She would take her little car down Banjo Mountain, sit for a spell, probably cry till the tears stopped, then come back.

'Then you're still keeping it on?' asked Bruce.

'Keeping what on?'

'Your flat, Clemmie.' Again he was puzzled.

'Oh, yes. I never intended to take up permanent residence here.'

'You mean live with your people?'

'Yes.'

'You don't like it?'

'On the contrary, I think it's the most perfect spot I've ever seen.'

'Oh, good, then. Do you know, Clemmie, I don't think I could bear it here if *you* didn't like it.'

'How couldn't I like it?' Clemmie said warmly, though really she was tingling with an almost frozen elation. He didn't think he could bear it if she didn't like it! That sounded at though—as if—— But what was the use? Amber was coming home.

'Will you walk up the hill with me?' Bruce was asking her.

'No, I intend to get away at once.'

'Wise, perhaps. It's getting on. Watch the night travellers. Shall I see you tomorrow?'

'Probably.' A pause. 'Probably you'll see my sister, too.'

'I asked about you,' he said firmly.

'Then you'll see me. I'll be the scrappy one.'

'An endearing scrap.'

'Bruce——' she began.

'But that's for moonlight and starry terraces, not for late afternoon and outside a bathroom door. All right, having been booted out, I'll go quietly. Only, Clemmie——'

'Yes, Bruce?'

'Take care, dear.'

Dear! She tasted that exquisitely for a moment.

'You mean lots of dogs would miss me?' she deliberately quirked.

'I mean—— Oh, damn, not outside a bathroom! Goodbye, then.' He grinned at her, and went down the passage. She heard him bid thanks and goodbye to her mother and stepfather. She saw him leave the house.

She turned, tears blurring her eyes, and went to her room. She did not wait for a secluded corner down the valley, but cried at once, cried hard and bitter and long, and later felt better.

She showered in the bathroom that Bruce had; she even intentionally reached for his damp towel. I love him, she knew, I love Bruce. He could love me, I think he does a little already, only it will never happen because of the crocodile who tastes but doesn't consume. Because of Amber. I can try and I can fight, but it still won't happen, or if it does, it will happen second place.

She dressed, looked for her parents to tell them she

was driving up the coast, could not find them, so left a note instead, then went out and got into her Mini.

Five minutes later she was taking the hairpin bends down to the shore highway to Brisbane.

It was glorious country, and at this quiet end of day almost hurting in its extravagant beauty. Clemmie drove past singing streams, palms and wild limes dressed up in staghorns and wild orchids and gemmed with flashing parakeets. The faintly blue coastal air grew bluer as dusk approached and the sea grew nearer, for the Pacific always spilled its blue everywhere, it was a spendthrift ocean.

She turned carefully into the main traffic stream, surprised and pleased at the meagre activity. People must be preparing for their evening meal, she decided, for the road was an important artery.

But now it was near-empty, and quite empty when Clemmie swung into the section that cut through the forest at Tallebudgera. She always loved this spot, trees everywhere, around, above, beside, only the bitumen intruding, and a sign that reminded you that you were intruding on nature. The sign said: 'Koalas cross here at night.' The warning was on behalf of the koalas, though a knock from them could also distract and upset a driver. However, not to worry, Clemmie grinned, she never yet had encountered a furry stranger.

Never? She pulled up with a squeal of indignant brakes. On the highway verge sat the biggest grey teddy bear she had seen in all her life.

One did not often meet such very large specimens, not outside their forest confines, for they were lazy stay-at-homes, and spent whatever time they weren't sleeping in eating, and this one was certainly plump evidence of that. They dozed through the day, ate at night, and Clemmie had a suspicion by the surprised look now in Billy Bluegum's round eyes that this was his very first adventure, and his wide girth the result of a treetop crib with an abundance of nearby leaves. I doubt, she smiled to herself, if he's even been ground-active all his life.

But he must have stirred himself this evening to have reached the bitumen from his particular tree, and he must also have been about to cross over. Or had he already crossed? Had he even crossed and been hit? For the first time Clemmie saw the car drawn further up on the road's shoulder, she saw a figure, a man's tall figure. He was quite near the koala.

She hurried forward.

'Is he hurt? Did you run over him? Why didn't you heed the notice and go slow? What are you doing with him? He's strictly protected, you know that, of couse?'

A deep, slightly bored, slightly amused, definitely long-suffering voice answered Clemmie, answered her concisely.

'No. No. I did. Nothing. Yes.'

'Then——?'

'I saw him but couldn't believe my eyes, so I stopped the car to make sure. Magnificent boy, isn't he?'

'Yes. Undoubtedly King Billy Bluegum, I'd say.'

'Do we bow?' he asked.

'Not too close if we do. The koala, unless used to being handled as in a park or reserve, has a very definite dignity. He wouldn't care for any spontaneous cheek-to-cheek.'

'Are you a reserve attendant?' the man asked.

'No, but I know about animals. I'm an assistant vet.' For the second time in an hour Clemmie had said that.

'Then I'll take your word—reluctantly.'

'I know,' nodded Clemmie, 'they're the cuddliest things. I only hope he doesn't try to cross. The traffic is non-existent now, but at any moment——'

'Then shall we encourage him back to his larder? Come on, old boy.'

Before Clemmie could protest, though she supposed she would not have protested, how otherwise could you send the woolly thing on its way without a nudge, the man had put out his hand. At once the koala climbed up his arm, no doubt thinking it was an accommodating gum, then, finding it less lofty than was to his liking, digging his teeth, to show his disgust, in the nearest branch ... which was the man's arm.

Those leaf-eating teeth could be very sharp, Clemmie knew that, and she did not wonder at the man's grunt and his prompt releasing of the bear.

But King Blue was not finished. Bumping to the ground in such a fashion was not at all to his liking. He turned and promptly dug his teeth into another branch ... the man's leg. This time there was more than a pained grunt, there was a yelp. It did the victim no good, but it certainly helped the attacker. It got him on his way. The koala turned and loped off. There was the cracking of parting branches, the sound of bark being scraped as something shinned up.

'Our visitor has gone,' sighed the man.

'And left,' added Clemmie, looking at his wounds, 'a few visiting cards. Painful ones, I'd say.'

'You'd say right. However, I've been bitten before.'

'By a koala?'

'No, but that labrador's teeth were equally sharp.'

'And were you previously immunised?'

'Tetanus, you mean? I can't recall precisely, I was a child.'

'Well, either you were injected or lucky. Are you now?'

'Lucky?' he queried.

'Injected? Protected?'

'No. I don't need to be. Then I lived on a farm, so I was at risk, now I'm a city slicker.'

'But still at risk. Am I to take it then that you're unprotected?'

'Yes, but I hardly think that Billy Bluegum——'

'Then think again.' Clemmie looked sternly at him.

'A fellow who lives on juicy gum tips?' the man objected. 'Don't you know about eucalyptus, then? It's a cure-all—my grandmother told me so. Chills, rheumatics, sore throats, stuffy noses——'

'Athletes' stiff joints,' nodded Clemmie, 'and I agree with Grandmother, but that was years ago, and now there's pollution. Forests aren't the same any more. These times science asks for more direct action. It has to.'

'You said you were a vet?' he queried.

'Assistant,' she corrected.

'Then I'm sure you know all about cats and dogs, but——'

'And cows, pigs, canaries, horses and wombats.'

'Really?' He cocked a brow at her.

'Really,' she said coolly.

'And your verdict?'

'Definitely immunisation,' she said firmly.

'Meaning a shot?'

'Yes.'

'Where?'

'Where? The usual spot, I expect.'

'I meant where do I go?'

'A hospital would be the best bet, a doctor might not have the necessary stuff on hand.'

He still hesitated. 'It's not to my liking to be advised by a vet,' he grinned.

'Assistant,' she corrected. 'But why not? Vets do as long a course as a doctor.'

'Point taken, but animal patients can bite back if the treatment hurts, and I can't.'

'Coward!'

'I always was,' he admitted, 'but this time perhaps I'll be brave. I have big business up this corner and it's important that I don't contact anything. Yes, I'll take your advice. Where do I drive?'

'The General Hospital will be the closest,' said Clemmie.

'Where's that?'

'You don't know!' Clemmie was incredulous, she thought everyone knew this Gold Coast.

He explained, 'I'm a sandgroper.'

'Sandgroper?' she queried.

'A West Australian. I come when I'm needed to Brisbane, but this is my first visit here. It's essential that I attend to several concerns tomorrow, so if you don't mind me following you——'

The last words were not said very distinctly, Clemmie detected a slight blur in the enunciation. She looked covertly at him and saw him waver. He was having a reaction, a small one, perhaps, but even a slight unawareness was too much when you were driving a car.

'You can't follow me,' she said, 'you're not fit.'

'Give me five minutes.'

'That won't do, either, the shot should be afforded as soon as possible.'

'I'll be all right,' he assured her.

'If I do the driving you will.'

'I said I'd be all right.' He stuck out an obstinate chin; he would, thought Clemmie, be an obstinate person.

'We'll go in my car,' she continued, as though he had not interrupted, 'your own car will be safe where you've parked it, it's well off the road. Mine, on the other hand, is on the road. I got out in a hurry.'

'No,' he inserted.

'Also,' Clemmie persisted, 'I doubt if I could drive yours.'

'I——'

'There won't be as much room in Miss Muffett——'

'Miss Muffett?' he queried.

'She's a little model,' Clemmie explained.

'Like you,' he commented.

'There won't be as much room in her, but you should fit in. I have, on occasion, even carried a small donkey.'

'Won't a big one be too much?'

'You never let me finish. A donkey *and* a dog. A substantial retriever.'

'I give in.' He let her push him into the seat beside the driver. Clemmie went round to the driving position and they set off.

She drove as quickly as she could to Southport Hospital, much quicker than she cared about, for the evening traffic had started, but she felt, in spite of the man's determined conversation, that talk was the last thing he really desired or would have been advised. When she reached the clinic she lost no time in getting him to Casualty, and though she did not actually assist him, for she felt he would not stand for that, she did walk very close, and her hand was ready.

However, he managed it all unaided, and was whisked off for dressings and shots.

Ten minutes later he was discharged, a little pale but evidently fit to let go.

'Get some rest,' the young resident advised.

'I'll do that.' The man followed Clemmie back to Miss Muffett.

'Where to?' Clemmie asked.

'Where to?'

'Where to for that rest?'

'Oh, anywhere,' he shrugged. 'The first pub or motel.'

'But which pub or motel?'

'The first.'

'I meant at which one have you booked? Your business is here, you said?'

'Yes.'

'Then where?' she persisted.

'Anywhere I can lay my head.'

'But you must know the name, or have the events confused you? Perhaps if you could let me see your booking.'

'No booking,' he said.

'What?'

'No booking.' He sighed. 'Look, what is this? I've been told that the hostelries along the Gold Coast match the population.'

'They do,' said Clemmie, 'but they don't match the visitors, not always, and this is one of those occasions. It's conference time, all the big hotels will be filled up.'

'Then make it a small hotel.' He spoke wearily.

'It is also,' said Clemmie, 'high season.'

'Then a motel, a flat, even a room. Some dive in a back street.'

'No dives here, but there are back streets. I'll try for you.' Clemmie turned the car.

At first he joined with her in trying to pinpoint a vacancy in the forest of electric signs that illuminated even the minor roads, then he became silent. Thinking he was discouraged at the No in front of every Vacancy, Clemmie looked obliquely at him, only to find he was asleep. Not just a tired slipping off but a solid sleep. Even if she found a vacancy she knew she would never be able to get him into the place, not in his present state. She must either pull up and let him sleep it off, or she must drive around until he came to.

She decided on the latter, and ten minutes later was on the way to Brisbane—an instinctive move, as she did it so often, but at the same time a wise one, she thought, as it should widen the possibility of an over-night stay for him. He could easily travel back to his conference in the morning.

What conference was it? she wondered idly as she drove along the dark bitumen. Who was he? What did he do?

She kept an eye open for a motel vacancy, but to no avail. Every one had its No lit up. Business was brisk tonight. And the man still slept.

An hour later Clemmie sighed and gave up. There was simply no accommodation anywhere. The only thing to do was to take him home to her own flat.

There was no difficulty as far as she was concerned; her parents, when she did not return, would know she had stayed overnight. She was glad now she had not given up the small pad, though she supposed she would have to now, that she was out of a job. No, the only difficulty would be getting him into the apartment. She supposed she could ask someone to help her, but she did not want to do that.

She was lucky. Just as she pulled up at the unit door, he opened his eyes.

'Found something,' he praised. 'Good girl.' He got out with her and followed her, a little drunkenly, into the digs.

He was rocking a little, and desperately in need of a bed, but before she lowered him into her single cot, only removing his shoes and coat and throwing over a light rug, he muttered: 'You managed to snare a good one. It looks more like a home than an overnight stop.'

'Yes. Now rest.' Clemmie saw that she need not have told him that, that he was asleep again already.

She tiptoed outside, looking ruefully at the armchair that was all that was offering for her own rest. Still, it was an emergency, and she was glad she had been able to help. In the morning she must check those Billy Bluegum wounds of his, see that they were showing no angry intent. Odd that within twelve hours she had medically treated two men when she had never previously treated any male ... only male pigs, horses, numerous dogs and cats ... in her life. Drought or famine, she grinned, no men or a crowd of them. Well, two at least.

She looked down at his jacket that she had brought out with her to arrange across the back of a chair. He would be rumpled enough at the lower end tomorrow without a crushed top as well. It was a good jacket, the kind of jacket an executive would wear to a conference. She draped it carefully.

It was then that the wallet fell out, and it didn't just fall, it opened and spilled its contents. No money, it was not that kind of wallet, but papers. Clemmie replaced them neatly, trying to put them in the order she believed they might have been.

During the replacing, a card caught her eye. It was not a visitor's card, not a commercial card, it was a personal card personally signed. It must belong to this man.

It read: Rickaby Roen.

Rickaby Roen! There would, thought Clemmie, be only one Rickaby Roen, the name was so—well, unlikely.

Rickaby Roen, she mused. So here was the extremely eligible male whom Amber had captured for herself. The parents had been very pleased about that; they had told Clemmie frequently how well Amber had done.

But the thing that puzzled Clemmie now, knowing her sister, was how R.R. was here and not under Amber's watchful eye. Also, why Amber was going home, but no mention of anyone going with her, especially any Rickaby Roen.

There could be lots of reasons ... this approaching conference, for instance. He might be calling up at Summer Heights Estate following that event.

But, and an irresistible giggle escaped Clemmie, how would Amber and the others take the news when they all met up that last night Rickaby Roen had slept at Clemmie's? How would they react to that?

Putting out the light, she cuddled up into the chair and hoped for oblivion. Her last thoughts were tangled ones. 'You see,' she heard herself explaining to the family, 'a koala bit him, so I had to take him in.'

Who, just who would believe such a tale?

But then the man's name was equally unbelievable. If you hadn't previously heard of it, or hadn't read it

on a personal card, could you possibly credit a Mr
Rickaby Roen?

'No,' Clemmie muttered, barely an inch off sleep.

When she opened her eyes again, it was morning,
the sun was buttering the windowsill, the curtains were
stirring slightly in the soft new air.

And Rickaby Roen stood there.

CHAPTER TWO

CLEMMIE spoke first. She said Hullo in a slightly tentative, slightly apprehensive voice, for Rickaby Roen looked anything but pleased.

He did not return the greeting, he demanded: 'Where in tarnation am I?'

'Somewhere near Brisbane.'

'Not the Gold Coast?'

'No, but don't worry, it will only take you an hour to get back.'

'In what?' he snapped.

'Taxi, or, if you prefer it, my car.'

'How did I come last night?' he asked.

'Don't you remember?'

'It's returning in bits, but it's very meagre. Somehow it has something to do with a bear.'

'Correctly you should say koala,' she explained. 'But yes, that's true. He bit you.' Clemmie added: 'Twice.'

'Hence my bandages?'

'Yes.'

'And my rather airy sensation?'

'That would be the shots,' she said, 'not King Blue.'

'Was I shot as well as bitten?'

'Yes, a tetanus shot. At the hospital.'

'Where do you come in?' he asked.

'At the time of the koala. I then drove you in for treatment, after which I searched for a unit for you but couldn't find any.'

'You found this,' he pointed out.

'Yes, but——'

'Yes, but it's not a motel unit, is that what you're going to say?'

Clemmie nodded.

'It's a flat. Your flat.'

'It had to be that or sleep in the car,' she explained, 'and you weren't in any condition to sleep in a car.'

'So you kidnapped me?'

'Can grown men be kidnapped?'

He was smiling now. He said: 'It certainly happened last night, and I thank you for ever. I believe you might even have saved my life.'

'Oh, no, koalas aren't fatal.'

He shrugged. 'A night in a car would have been. I'd already driven from Sydney in one hop. Twelve hundred kilometres takes it out of you.'

'It was my pleasure.' Clemmie had started to say her duty, then altered it. But pleasure, she thought, reddening, wasn't quite the word, either.

'It couldn't have been, not curled up in a chair.'

'It's a very large chair and I'm——'

'You're small time,' he nodded.

'I was going to say scrappy,' she said.

'No, you're not scrappy.'

'What time is your conference?' she asked.

'It's a convention, really.'

'Worse still.'

He raised his brows, and Clemmie explained: 'You're rumpled. I never took your clothes off.'

He raised his eyebrows. 'Do you usually?'

'There's no usually.' But as she said it, Clemmie remembered Bruce's trews, and she half-grinned.

'I don't know whether to believe the lady,' the man remarked, 'but I do agree with her about my crushed state. I'm hideously rumpled. The gathering is at ten. Would there be time for me to go back to my car ... oh, yes, I'm remembering it all now ... and get my bag?'

'No time, only time for coffee, then departure.'

'Oh.'

'But I could press your things,' she said. 'The shirt wouldn't be pristine, but no one would notice.'

'Would you do that?' he asked.

'I'm starting right now. You could take off your pants, too, and I'll press them.' Good heavens, this was uncanny, not only two physical repair jobs in a short time but two launderings!

'You can drape the rug around you' ... at least, thought Clemmie, she would not be repeating the dressing gown routine ... 'and while you're about it let me see those wounds.'

He did so, and she examined and passed them.

'OK for a dog?' he asked.

'And a man. Now for coffee.'

They had it on Clemmie's small verandah, the Brisbane River twisting like a silver snake beneath them.

He said this, and Clemmie assured him: 'A friendly snake, this is a friendly state.'

'Have you ever tended a snake?' he asked.

'Once we had a lizard.'

'We?'

'I mean my employer did,' she corrected.

'The vet?'

'Yes.'

'What time do you start work?' he asked. 'I mean, should you be wasting time on me now?'

'I'm put off,' she told him.

'Dismissed?'

'In a way.'

'You fed the canary to the——'

'No, I was very good, as a matter of fact. But unhappily the firm moved south.'

'So you're currently unemployed?'

'Yes.'

'Do you want a job?' he asked. 'I have branches everywhere, and it's the least I can do after all your kindness.'

'You mean you're one of those influential people who can summon up posts at a rub of a lamp?'

'No, I'm not Aladdin,' he replied.

She knew that already, she knew he was Rickaby Roen, but she also knew that in a modern world a big bank balance could achieve as much as a fabled lamp.

'I can't type,' she told him, 'and I add badly, and, anyway, I didn't do it for that.'

'Of course. I'm sorry.' He smiled at her and Clemmie smiled back.

'You look an outdoors man,' she told him, 'not a conference or convention or business type. You have red skin.'

'Of course. I'm a Red Indian. What else about me?'

'Tall, broad, quite nice.'

'Thank you,' he said. 'Now my turn for you, though as if you did not know.'

'Know what?'

'That you're lovely.'

'Oh, no!' Clemmie was positively startled. 'I've never been that.'

'Then I have news for you.' His smile this time was warm and sincere.

'I haven't, though, my sister got all the goodies. By

the way, I'm glad that I did what I did even apart from doing it out of duty.'

'The original word was pleasure,' he said. 'But go on.'

'I'm glad I did it, because in a way we're—related.'

'What?'

'Related.'

'I've never seen you before in my life!'

'And I haven't seen you, but we're still related, or will be.'

'I'm all agog,' he said. 'Can I be included in this?'

'You are included—I just told you.'

'I mean can I be told how?'

'I found it out last night when I hung up your jacket,' she explained.

'Yes. Thank you for that.'

'I found out about you,' Clemmie repeated.

'I suppose you mean the Summer Heights Estate project,' he shrugged. 'I brought along all the papers.'

'The what?' She looked at him in complete surprise.

'Summer Heights Estate. As a resident of Brisbane you must have heard of that promotion.'

'Of course I've heard of it.'

'Then I'm buying in. That's what I've *really* come up here for. My Queensland branch could have handled the convention, but this other needed a personal touch. Summer Heights, according to what I've been told, is a promotion *extraordinaire*, the kind of thing I like, the kind of thing I go after . . . and get.'

'But how can you buy in? I mean, it's strictly limited. It's in the tight possession of Malling, Fitzroy and Osborne.' Clemmie gulped a little over Malling.

'You seem to know a lot about it,' he observed.

'As you said, it's a promotion *extraordinaire,* and everyone is interested in those kind of things.'

'Have you seen it?' he asked.

'Yes.'

'Is it worthy?'

She smiled. 'It's beautiful.'

'I see. Then Fitzroy isn't cheating me with this price.'

She looked at him incredulously. 'He's selling out to you?'

Rickaby Roen nodded. 'He couldn't resist the price. By tonight I'll own his thirty-three and a third per cent.'

'Only a third. You still won't own the company.'

'When I get Osborne's third I practically will.'

'You mean you'll have two-thirds to the Malling one-third?'

'My arithmetic comes out the same,' he nodded.

'You sound confident.'

'I always am because I always win.'

She was silent a while. 'Then what?' she asked at length.

'The usual—buy out the remaining name. In this instance Malling. I don't know Malling though I have heard of him, but I do know me, and I'm not the easiest of partners to work with, nor to defeat. Oh, yes, I think he'll come round.' He must have seen a look on her face. 'That's business. Any objection?'

'No. I mean, how could I have?'

'Well, you might have if you were, as you say you are, a relation. You might be thinking to yourself: "How will all this affect me?" Which brings me to an important point. What precisely are you? A stepsister of a second aunt, something out of *Pinafore*?'

'Not even that close,' said Clemmie. 'Not yet.'

'You intrigue me,' he drawled.

'My name might help, then. It's Green.'

He shrugged. 'Not unique.'

'What about—Amber Green?'

'Amber Green?' He looked honestly puzzled; he was a good actor.

'Amber Green,' Clemmie said again.

'Come again?'

'She worked ... works ... well, I don't know how it is now ... in your Brisbane branch.'

'Which I attend only rarely. But something is breaking. Amber Green.' He thought hard, then gave Clemmie a long look.

'Where do you come in?' he asked.

'We're sisters.'

'Meaning?'

'Well, you and Amber are—well, not yet exactly, but you will be—which makes me—well, it makes me——'

'Continue, please.'

'Your future sister-in-law.'

'*What?*' he said in astonishment.

'You heard me.'

'Yes, I did, but—but—— Well, perish the thought,' he said firmly.

Instantly, before she could answer him, or drop her lip, or anything at all, he assured her: 'I don't mean it like it sounds.'

'You mean you don't wish to imply perish the thought of me being your sister-in-law?'

'Oh, I do mean that, I can think of a far better relationship. No, and you're going to despise me for this, but nonetheless it has to be said: *Perish the thought of Amber ever having broadcast such a thing.'*

'She didn't,' said Clemmie, 'she just told my mother and stepfather.'

'Broadcast,' he said again. 'It's untrue. Nothing even began as far as I'm concerned.'

'She's beautiful.'

'I'll take your word.'

'But you have eyes,' she persisted.

'Yes, I have eyes.' He set his own eyes, dark eyes, but a red gleam in them somewhere, the same as his skin and his hair had red gleams, on Clemmie.

'There was never anything,' he repeated. 'You must believe me.'

'But——' she began.

'The only thing there could have been was wishful thinking—on *her* part. If that sounds boastful, I'm sorry, but it's still meant.'

'Amber never wishes, she achieves,' Clemmie stated.

'Well, she hasn't achieved this time, has she? Anyway, why should she wish for me?'

'Money?' she suggested.

'Yes, I have that, but quite a few men have.'

'At your attractive age? With your appearance? For you're youngish and very attractive, you know.'

'Thank you, sister *not*-to-be. More coffee?' He took her cup and refilled it. 'Having straightened out that relationship,' he drawled when he handed it back, 'what else?'

'Well—— Summer Heights. We live there, you see—I mean, my parents do. I'm going back there to-day, and when I reach home Amber will have come home as well. I—I thought she would be bringing *you*.'

'She won't, and after what you've told me I won't be travelling up myself even to look over the place. I'll take Fitzroy's word. But what about your parents? Will your father produce a shotgun?'

'Stepfather,' she corrected.

'Amber's, too?'

'Yes, we were two precious gems who came with Mother's second marriage.'

'A broken first marriage?' he asked.

'You want to know a lot.'

'Yes,' he admitted, 'I do.' He seemed a little surprised with himself and his interest.

'Our father died, and Amber was born after his death. I guess it was all too awful for Mother, for she married—quite soon. She married a Daryl Coyle. He has made her very happy.'

'Then why are you sad?' he asked.

'Am I? I mean—I'm not.'

'You are, though. Why?'

She looked at him a little piteously. Since Aunt Mary, her father's sister, had passed on, she seemed to have had no one to talk to. She had felt she could talk to Bruce, she had been *sure* she could talk to Bruce, but after today that would be all over. Amber would be there.

'Why?' he persisted.

'I've always felt sad ... no, hollow is the word ... for Father.'

'Your own father?'

'Yes.'

'Can you remember him?'

'I was only three.'

'They say that memory begins from then,' he told her.

'He was much older than Mother ... of course I can't recall that, but I've been told.'

'So your mother does speak about him?'

'Oh, no, my Aunt Mary told me. She told me all I do know, but that's very little, because Aunt Mary isn't ... wasn't the telling sort. But she did tell me about the awful thing.'

'What awful thing?'

'We were in a boat on a lake. The others had got off, but Father and I were still in the boat. Something happened, one of those things that do occur in boats, I expect, and we tipped over. My father saved me, but before they—the people on the bank—could haul him in as well, he slipped back, and—well, he drowned.'

'I see.'

'Amber was coming, and Mother married almost at once after the birth. Everyone said it was the best thing to do.'

'Did Aunt Mary say it?'

'She said not many men would have accepted an instant family.'

'Wise Aunt Mary,' he drawled.

'Yes.' A pause. 'I miss her.' All at once, and to her horror, for he was no relation, and wasn't going to be, Clemmie began to cry.

He let her cry. Several times he patted her shoulder, but he let her cry herself out.

'If you've finished,' he said factually at last, 'I wonder if we could leave? Or would you prefer me to leave in a taxi to allow you to finish the final tear?'

'It's done. I'm dried out.' She smiled tremulously. 'Oh, I must be growing into a weeping Winifred!'

'Is that your name?'

'No. Anyway, I must be a desert now. It's the second

time I've cried in twenty-four hours.' She had done several things twice recently, Clemmie thought, she had attended a man's wounds, looked after a man's clothes.—Cried.

'Why did you cry before?' he probed. 'And what's your name?'

'Clemmie. Clementine.'

'And the tears?'

She shrugged. 'Oh—nothing.'

'You don't look the sort to cry over nothing to me.'

'All right then,' she sighed. 'I cried because Amber was coming.'

'Cried for happy? I was up in New Guinea once and they used to say that, cry for happy.'

'No, I cried for sad ...' Suddenly he was Aunt Mary, dead Aunt Mary, not really, of course, not this Red Indian of a man, but a wall on which to wail.

'Yes, Clemmie?'

'You see, I'd met—Bruce. He's our new neighbour.'

'Go on,' he said gently.

'He's ... well——'

'You're trying to tell me you like him?'

'Yes.'

'You like him very much?'

'Yes.'

'And you're frightened that Amber——'

'Yes,' she sighed.

'Then you're a fool. Are you ready or not?'

'Ready.' Clemmie got up.

At the door she said: 'You're only being helpful, aren't you? You're grateful about last night so you're being kind.'

'No, I was saying what I felt. Of course I don't know this Bruce——'

'Bruce *Malling*.'

'Malling? One of the Malling, Fitzroy and Osborne trio?'

'Yes.'

'One of my hills to be conquered?'

'If you put it that way,' sighed Clemmie.

'I do. Malling, eh! Now we are getting involved, aren't we?'

'How?' she asked.

'I'll be frank with you. It's all not quite so casual as I might have made it sound before. I've definitely come up here this time with one express purpose—not the convention, but the business after. The Summer Heights business. I've come to buy out Fitzroy, later Osborne, and after that I eat up Malling.'

'If you can,' she put in.

'Oh, I can.'

'If he'll let himself get eaten.'

'He'll need a lot of what it takes to stop intact.'

'You're ruthless,' Clemmie said.

'Business men are.'

'Bruce isn't,' she insisted.

'Then he'll fall by the wayside, won't he, which should suit you admirably, you're good at administering fellow comfort. But what' . . . a thin smile . . . 'about Amber?'

'How do you mean?'

'What will she think *then* of her supposedly promising candidate?'

'You're horrible!' she said angrily.

'For helping *your* cause? For I will be helping it, my dear. The little I saw of your sister whenever I went to Brisbane soon convinced me she would have no time for lame dogs.'

'Bruce isn't that, and he won't be,' she said firmly.

'You're wrong, for he surely will be, poor fellow. You see I *am* ruthless, just as you said. Also I'm very well equipped—financially I mean. But why fret? *You* will be around to pick up the pieces when your sister finds she has no inclination for a second best.'

She said firmly, 'Bruce is no second best.'

'Really?' He gave a rather bored shrug. 'I can scarcely wait to meet my new partner.'

'To consume him? I'm going back that way anyhow, or I'd leave you to take a taxi after all, but seeing that I'm travelling down ...'

She said those last words to nothing. The man had swung away from her, had descended the last step, crossed the road. She saw him hail a cab, talk with the driver and evidently come to an arrangement, as it was over an hour's journey. She saw him get in.

He did not look back at her, which made it rather an anticlimax. She had saved him, or so he had said, and though that was an exaggeration she had expected more than a turned away head.

One thing, she thought, getting into her Mini, the adventure had achieved one thing: Until this morning, until only a little time ago, she had not even thought of Bruce and Amber. The pain that had seemed large enough to fill eternity had left her so completely it might never have been there at all.

It was only when Clemmie turned into the drive of the house on the Summer Heights Estate that it all returned.

A car was drawn up—Amber's smart red sports car. Her mother, seeing her, came out on to the patio and called: 'At last! I was wondering when you would come. I'll need your help. Amber is home and we've asked Bruce Malling down for dinner. That makes three extra ... I'm counting you now ... and it's rather a tall order when I'm accustomed to only two.'

'Hands across the table,' nodded Clemmie, coming in. She knew something flippant like that was expected of her.

'Clementine, can't you be serious for once?'

Oh, I'm serious, Clemmie thought, I've never been more serious in my life, but I mustn't show it. For Bruce's sake I mustn't show it. I love Bruce, and if preferring Amber, and it seems the stage is being set for that, is what is to happen, then I hope everything goes right for him. Most of all, *most of all* I don't want Bruce hurt.

Clemmie helped her mother with the table arrangement. She noted that the best of everything was being laid out. She also noted that the library door was closed, and once, when the sound of voices drifted out, her mother said: 'Amber is talking with Father.'

If she had been talking of Clementine, Clemmie knew, Alison would have said: 'Clementine is talking with her stepfather.' It had always been thus, partly because Amber had been a baby when she came with the marriage, Clemmie supposed, but more because ... well, because Mr Coyle had always favoured Amber. How could he have done otherwise, Clemmie often had asked herself, Amber had been much prettier, much more amusing, and she had accepted her stepfather as though he was her own parent. She had trilled Father ... Daddy ... Dad right from babyhood, something that Clemmie never had done.

'What's the matter with me?' Clemmie had once asked Aunt Mary. 'I can't, like Amber, say what I know I should to Mr Coyle.

'Amber knew no one else,' said Aunt Mary.

'Neither did I, I mean not very much. I can only remember a big hand to hold on to.'

'Then don't let that big hand blot out the worthiness of Daryl Coyle. He must have been worthy to have taken on such responsibility.' But Aunt Mary had recited more than said it.

'You don't like him, either,' Clemmie recalled herself discovering triumphantly.

'You silly child, I feel nothing at all, I'm not expected to.'

'Am I?' asked Clemmie.

'He took over your care.'

Clemmie begged, 'I wish you'd tell me everything, Aunt Mary.'

'There's nothing to tell that you don't know already. There was the boating accident, then your mother remarried. A very wise thing under the circumstances.'

'But they never look like that.'

'Who doesn't? And look like what?'

'Alison and Daryl. Look under the circumstances. They look—in love.'

Aunt Mary, Clemmie remembered, had glanced at her sharply, spoken to her sharply.

'You should be pleased about that.'

'Are you?'

'You're a naughty little girl,' Aunt Mary had said sternly. 'I'm annoyed with you.'

'Why won't you tell me?' Clemmie persisted.

'I was away. I've always been away more than at home.'

'Writing your wild life books. Stepfather said once the animals must be in our blood.'

'True. Your father was very keen on them.'

'And you. And now me. But not Amber.'

'No,' Aunt Mary had said in such a low voice that Clemmie barely had heard.

For all her father's sister's astringency, though, Clemmie always had adored Aunt Mary, had loved to visit her, had yearned to stop on.

'You're very attracted to your aunt,' her stepfather had remarked only last year.

'Yes, I am.'

'With an inheritance in view?' He had made a quirk of it, but his eyes had been narrowed.

'Aunt would have no money.'

'Yet some authors are reputed to be making excellent money.'

'Mystery writers, romantic ones,' she corrected, 'not wild life observers.'

'All the same ... I only hope you're not trying to undermine Amber, Clementine.'

'Amber never visits Aunt,' she pointed out.

'So you *are* undermining her.'

'No. I told you Aunt would have no money.'

He had ignored that. 'In all fairness your aunt should leave everything she has to your mother, though in my care, Alison, as a woman, being less knowledgeable on such things. Only then can justice be done.'

'Justice?' queried Clemmie.

'I did take over a big responsibility, remember.'

'Oh, I know, Aunt Mary has often told me so.'

'She has, has she? Well, you might take a leaf from her book.'

'What do you mean?'

'See things fairly, Clementine. I don't think you've ever tried.'

'Then I will. I'll tell Aunt Mary you expect her to leave her money to you.'

'I didn't say that,' said Daryl.

'Then to Mother, but in your jurisdiction.'

'I trust you have better sense than that, a better way of expressing things,' Daryl had said coldly. 'I only spoke because I had noticed the number of times you've been visiting Mary Green, and wondering if it was because of her advancing years.'

Clemmie said, 'She's young at heart.'

'Not quite good enough, I'm afraid. Time takes its inevitable toll.' Daryl had got up. 'But this is a distasteful conversation. I wonder how you came to bring it up.'

'I didn't. I——' But what was the use? Daryl had left.

Clemmie had quite unashamedly repeated the conversation to Mary on her next visit, she always had told her aunt everything.

'The man is right,' Mary had shrugged, 'and I'll bequeath everything to Alison with Daryl as executor as he said. I only wish I could be here and see his face when he sees how little it is. Though I supose undivided, as it will be then, it will seem more. You do understand me, Clemmie? I would be leaving nothing at all personally to you. They'd never forgive it.'

'Neither would I forgive it, I don't want you ever to go.'

Aunt Mary had smiled.

'I'll leave you my musical box and you can think of me every time you play it. Winter Wonderland! An odd liking in this country of summer! Will that do you? You always loved it.'

'Don't talk about these things,' begged Clemmie.

'I'm finished with them now, but you could drop a word to the worthy Daryl.'

Clemmie had done so that night.

'Very satisfactory,' he had nodded, 'I'm pleased with the rightness of it, pleased you spoke to her.' It had been perhaps the first commendation Clemmie ever had had from Daryl, and she had stood silent.

'You'll be looked after,' he had finished graciously, 'never fear.'

A few weeks later Aunt Mary had died, and now her estate was being wound up. Mr Coyle knew the general trend of the will, and he had smiled condescendingly over Clemmie's inheritance.

'A musical box! Still, none of us are getting all that much. Why didn't Mary write something popular?'

'She preferred animals,' Clemmie had murmured, and had known in that moment that she did, too.

Now she looked at the closed library door, heard but did not follow the lowered voices.

'You've put the forks on the wrong side,' Alison Coyle complained. 'Really, Clementine, can't you do anything?'

Eventually Amber emerged from her talk with Daryl and joined Clemmie in the bedroom they shared.

'Hi,' she greeted.

'Hullo, Amber. Nice to see you again.'

'Not so nice for the folk.' Amber nodded in the library direction.

'They always want to see you,' Clemmie assured her.

'But they would have preferred me holding on to a millionaire.'

'Only for your sake.'

'Yes, I think you're right,' sighed Amber. 'Well, it just didn't come off.'

'Did you expect it to?'

'He took me out, but I've learned since he does that to all his new employees whenever he visits any of his branches.'

'Beautiful or not?' nodded Clemmie.

Typical of Amber, she did not argue that, and how could she have argued, when she was, and knew it, a perfectly lovely woman.

'He would have been a feather in my cap ... isn't that an absurd phrase? ... but no go. Rickaby Roen isn't the marrying sort.'

'Rickaby Roen?' Clemmie felt false looking unknowing like this.

'That was his name,' said Amber. 'I became one of his branch secs whenever he hit Brisbane. Oh, yes, the man had several secretaries. Social side, business side, internal side, external. But my goal was the matrimonial side, but no go. The sound he most dislikes, it seems, is wedding bells. Anyway, off with the old love, that never was, anyhow, and on with the new—or so I hope. Name of Bruce Malling. Stepfather has intimated that you two already have met.' She looked slyly at Clemmie.

'Yes,' said Clemmie briefly.

'Then I'm sorry if I'll be treading on your toes, darling, but a girl has to look to her future.'

'At eighteen!'

'Undoubtedly you didn't look at eighteen,' Amber observed, 'because see where you are at twenty-one.'

Clemmie sighed, 'Amber, you're impossible!'

'I know, but doesn't it suit me?' The girl spread herself luxuriously, and yes, she was more than beautiful,

she was provocation, enticement, allure, desire, she was
life itself.

Clemmie sighed again.

'But on the subject of looks, you're not looking too
bad yourself, old Clem,' Amber went on.

... After sleeping all night on a chair! Clemmie
shuddered. After all that had happened since yesterday
when Stepfather had announced: 'Amber is coming
home.'

'How do you mean?' she asked. 'I'm the same.
Rather tired, as a matter of fact.'

'I dunno,' Amber said thoughtfully. 'No, I don't
really, Clem, but somehow you look——well, awakened.'

'Awakened? I could do with a good night's sleep.' It
was on the tip of Clemmie's tongue to explain why,
but Amber spoke first.

'A something not to do with looks,' she continued,
'an—an awareness that you're not aware of yourself.'

'You surprise me, Amber.'

'With my perception?'

'With your imaginings.'

Amber grinned, and let that pass.

'Tonight we're having for dinner a something called
Bruce Malling,' she mused.

'That sounds as though you're going to eat him!'
smiled Clemmie.

'Which would be a change—I certainly never got
round to eating Rickaby Roen! I'm going to look my
best, Clemmie, and if it pays results, then I'm sorry
about you, dear, but a girl has to think of herself.
Father hinted he could be quite a catch.' Amber
stretched, crossed to the en suite bathroom and turned
on a tap.

'Sorry, Clem,' she tossed as she pulled the shower door.

Clemmie changed mechanically, making do with a splash in the basin while Amber still lingered in the recess. When she came out she put on the first dress that came to hand. What use would it have been to do otherwise? Even if you spent a lifetime and a fortune, Amber still would steal the scene.

She slipped out of the room before Amber emerged from the bathroom; she had had enough of Amber for a while. She went quietly, secretly out to the patio.

Secretly? The moment she emerged Bruce Malling stepped forward.

'Clemmie! What luck! I arrived early and didn't want to walk in yet.'

'You could have, Bruce,' she smiled.

'Let me finish. I came early in the hope of seeing you and now I am seeing you. This is just what I wished for.'

'Why?' Clemmie could not have said why she was acting this way.

'I wanted to talk to you before we went in, before I met your sister, before——'

'You won't say that afterwards,' she assured him.

He was not heeding her interruptions. He asked: 'Why didn't you tell me you weren't coming home last night? My call came early and I rushed down at once. Clemmie, I was very let down. We could have driven to the coast together. We could have done a lot of things.'

... *I* did, Clemmie thought.

Aloud she said: 'I'm sorry, Bruce, but you did tell me you had that call.'

'Yes, and it was prompt, as I said.' He sounded like a disappointed little boy.

'A good call, I hope.'

'I hope so. I was speaking to one of my partners—Osborne, as a matter of fact. He told me that our third partner, Fitzroy, was thinking of selling, but he seemed sanguine that Fitzroy would do nothing until we'd all conferred. That suited me. I intend to bid high for Fitzroy's third. I intend to outbid Osborne. I like Osborne, but I'd like him better if I held the controls.'

'Perhaps someone else will bid,' said Clemmie. 'Some outsider.'

'It would have to be a larger figure than I would offer. After all, Fitzroy has been with us for years. No, I think there's little doubt that Fitzroy will sell to me.'

'I see,' Clemmie said a little uncertainly; she was hearing another confident ... more confident ... voice.

'I don't think you do, Clemmie. I came down here all lit up, all ready to celebrate ... beforehand, perhaps, but pretty sure for all that ... and you weren't here, and you didn't even come back. I hung round, up at my own house, of course for hours. Clemmie, where were you?'

'At my flat.'

'Your Brisbane flat?'

'Yes.'

'Why did you go up there?'

'I had mail to pick up. I told you all this before, Bruce. Then I found I was too tired to come back. Oh, for goodness' sake, do we have to go on and on?'

'I'm sorry, Clemmie, but I was so disappointed. I wanted to tell you——'

'Now you've told me.'

'But I haven't asked you——'

What Bruce would have asked, Clemmie was never told, for at that moment Alison Coyle came out on the terrace, saw Bruce and insisted that the pair of them come in for drinks.

Clemmie followed Bruce into the dining room. She was puzzled at the feeling inside of her. It was not the feeling she had dreaded, not the hollowness, not the despair. She had expected when Amber walked in, which would be within a few moments, that her world would totter, but just now it was not like that at all. She simply stood waiting for the grand entry, as though she was someone sitting in the theatre stalls.

Then Amber came in.

Daryl Coyle was talking to Bruce, Alison was correcting one of Clemmie's spoons, Clemmie was just standing there.

Amber came in, and with her more beauty, Clemmie knew, than Bruce ever had imagined.

Clemmie looked across at Bruce as he held his glass aloft ... and a trifle crooked ... as he watched the approaching girl. Then she looked at Daryl Coyle, also looking at Amber. Then her stepfather turned his gaze from Amber and looked instead at Clemmie, and in the look Clemmie recognised triumph and dislike.

She had been conscious of her stepfather's dislike before. Even when he had said to people: 'My dear wife brought two precious gems to our marriage,' he had meant only one gem. Clemmie had known that. But never before had she encountered this unveiled dislike quite so much.

It was gone now, in fact it had disappeared so quickly it never might have flicked across his face at all. It could have been her imagination.

Daryl Coyle was quite graciously including Clemmie in the conversation—not the easiest of conversations, for Bruce was barely participating; he was visibly stunned, there was no other word for it, by Amber. He replied sparsely, but that did not disturb Daryl; he went calmly on until Alison suggested they sit down and eat.

The meal was like a dream to Clemmie—the well-appointed table, the quiet exchange of talk, the soft background music; Bruce doing the expected things and making the right moves but performing automatically.

At last it was over, and the women rose, while Daryl, a determined stickler, led Bruce into the library.

'I have the decanter here,' he called back, 'if you'll bring in the coffee.'

It fell to Clemmie to take in the coffee. She had stacked the dishes in the machine while Alison had perked the brew. Amber had disappeared, probably to make herself even more beautiful, if that was possible.

'It was a complete success,' Alison was purring.

'If you mean Bruce Malling did the expected, yes, you're right.'

'Really, Clementine!' A pause, then awkwardly: 'Clementine, it—it didn't matter to you, did it?'

'What, Mother?'

'Tonight. I mean——'

'You mean Bruce, don't you, Mother?' said Clemmie quietly.

'Well——'

'Of course it didn't matter. You must have seen for yourself yesterday that the only thing we had in common were four feet, and even then I really suspect the interest was only assumed on Bruce's part.'

'My breezy Clementine!' Alison spoke with relief, glad to salve her conscience so easily. She finished the coffee and asked Clemmie to take it in.

Without the presence of Amber, Bruce must have found himself able to converse once more. He was telling Daryl about the Malling ambition to change his company into one personal name, make Summer Heights Estate a strictly Malling promotion. Daryl was very enthusiastic, you could buy no better than S.H., he said. He nodded to Clemmie to put the coffee down, and asked Bruce if he had any concrete hopes.

'I have. Fitzroy is willing to sell his third, and I'm confident he'll sell to me,' said Bruce. 'With two-thirds of the entirety——' Bruce smiled and spread his hands.

Amber came out, and the ladies joined the men. The evening went on as dinner had. Small conversation and Bruce dazzled again.

At last Bruce rose and said he must leave, that tomorrow he had to see his partner.

'Perhaps by tomorrow night your late partner,' smiled Daryl.

Clemmie wondered a little hysterically what both men would have said if she had broken in with a cryptic: 'I wouldn't bet on that.'

She did not see Bruce out, but then neither did Amber, though Amber, being Amber, would be up to all these tricks, she would be very conscious of overexposure. Bruce would be kept on tenterhooks, he would never be laundered, bathed, anointed; only naïve people like Clemmie did things like that.

The next morning Bruce came down the hill to ask Clemmie could she look at one of the mares who had gone lame. He himself looked at Amber as he said it, an Amber more golden, more beautiful than ever in the keen morning light.

'At a fee, of course, Clemmie,' he said.

'I was only an assistant,' she insisted. 'I never passed

any qualifying exams, so I can't charge you.'

'*I* would charge you,' came in Amber impudently. She was standing beside Clemmie and when they walked up the hill she went, too.

'I would pay you,' Bruce came quickly back.

There was an uncomfortable silence, uncomfortable for Clemmie. Bruce, becoming conscious of her again, shrugged ruefully at both girls.

'Not that I'll be throwing any money around. I've had rather unpleasant news. I was speaking to Mr Coyle last night, telling him how I hoped to buy out one of my partners. Indeed, I felt sure Fitzroy would agree.'

'He didn't?' Amber asked.

'Someone else got in first. I've just been in touch with Brisbane, and it was while I was looking sadly at the estate that's not going to be as much mine as I thought that I noticed Polly's lameness. Yes, Fitzroy was got at by another bidder, someone with an offer so attractive Fitzroy closed the deal at once. If I could have pulled this thing off I would have held two-thirds of the entirety. As it is I'm still where I was.'

'The mare's foot is all right,' Clemmie came in. 'It's only a stone bruise. I'd rest her if I were you.'

'Will do that, Doctor,' Bruce promised.

'Why did a bachelor build a house like this?' Amber was asking. 'It's lovely, of course, but it's a family home.'

'That's what I had in mind.' Bruce spoke in a low voice; he seemed to have forgotten his disappointment, and he was looking at Amber.

Feeling suddenly definitely a third, Clemmie put the mare's leg back on the turf, got up and touched the soft head, then went down the hill again. She doubted if either Bruce or Amber saw, or heard, her go. She wondered if Amber always got her men like this, by giving them her rapt attention, her starry attention, like she was giving Bruce now. But still it hadn't succeeded with one of the men, with Rickaby Roen. Bruce had not mentioned Rickaby's name as the buyer of Fitzroy's shares. Perhaps he did not know that yet, only that his chance had gone. Poor Bruce, he really was sweet, even though ...

Clemmie kicked at a tuft of grass. If only I could get away, she thought suddenly, away from watching this thing between Amber and Bruce unfold. Standing by is going to be—to be——

No, not pain, she found in surprise, not resentment, just something I know the ending to already so don't want to wait until the finale.

If only Lindsay would send for me! I know he will once he gets established, but when, when?

As if in answer to her thoughts, her mother handed her two letters when she entered the house.

'Mail's come, dear. That looks as though it could come from your old firm, the postmark is Sydney, and you know no one else there.'

Clemmie tore the letter open eagerly, but a quick glance dashed her hopes at once.

'Lindsay writes that he's given up the idea of going it alone,' she told Alison, 'it's a big outlay, and anyway, he's had an attractive offer from the university.'

'Oh.' Alison stood disappointed for a moment.—— Disappointed for whom? 'Never mind, you might get something on the coast.'

'Trimming poodles. That's all that is open to me in my line down there,' Clemmie sighed.

'Then you'll have to do clerical or reception work.'

'I haven't been trained clerically, and one look at me and a patient——'

'I'm sure you play yourself down too much. That's a big fault with you, Clementine. What is the other letter?'

'An attractive offer from someone up here who's been panting for my services ever since Lindsay closed, no doubt.'

Even as she said it in disgust, Clemmie gasped. She had opened the letter, and it was almost as if she had X-ray eyes.

'Dear Miss Green, I have recently learned that you are at present between jobs, that your former employer has moved south. I am urgently in need of an assistant, versed, though not necessarily qualified, in vet knowledge and practice, for a small stud I have acquired. This stud, name of Sperry, is in Glen Tally, and well within reach, as you would know, of the coast, so you could either sleep in or sleep away, according to your preference.

'If you are interested, and I do hope you will be, perhaps you could come out to Glen Tally and examine the set-up. I believe you would know which road to take, but if there's any uncertainty, ask for the old Sperry Stud.

'Hoping to see you, hoping to sign you up——'

Clemmie could not decipher the signature, it was obliterated by a now redundant Sperry Stud stamp.

'What is it, Clementine?' her mother was asking.

'An offer. It sounds attractive. My own work, so at least I would be on knowledgeable ground. Also, although I'd be away, I'd still be up here—Queensland, I mean. I could even keep on my flat.'

Without waiting for any comment, though Alison

would have had only encouraging things to say, Clemmie went inside and pulled out her bag.

But before she packed, she sat at the window a while, staring up the hill to the Malling house.

A family home is what I had in mind. She heard Bruce saying it again ... and looking at Amber.

Presently Clemmie got up and began to fold her clothes.

CHAPTER THREE

CLEMMIE left after breakfast the next morning. She supposed she could have consulted the telephone book, found the number of the old Sperry Stud, contacted the new owner before she met him, asked him some pertinent questions, but in that way she might have been discouraged from starting, something she did not want, for she was determined to leave here as soon as she could. In fact it had become absolutely imperative that this happen at once. She could not, would not, watch this thing between Bruce and her sister come to fruition. She could not bear it.

There had been no demur from the family. Her mother already had shown her eagerness, and silence from her stepfather Clemmie took as satisfaction. That left Amber, and Amber, for the first time in Clemmie's memory, seemed unaware of things.

'Going?' she murmured absently to her sister when she saw the bags.

'Yes.'

'Have fun.'

'Amber, I'm going after a job,' Clemmie laughed.

'Mmm.' Amber was looking through the window up to Bruce's house, she was looking with deep absorption. Surely Amber was not—— No, Amber was incapable of——

Clemmie had closed her bags and gone. She had left Summer Heights Estate ... 'the finest and loveliest realty Australia can offer' ... said the ad that had won

Daryl Coyle ... and descended to the coastal flats. She rimmed several canals, crossed the Nerang River, ran beside a long gold beach, through the forest where she had been stopped by a koala and a man that eventful night, then, escaping the multi-rise with its resultant dense traffic of Surfers Paradise, she turned into another corner of the hinterland, quite steep hills this time, and beyond them the stud country of Southern Queensland, offering the same essential minerals and crystal lushness of the blue grass of America, the same ideal conditions for the raising of blue ribbon stuff.

As she drove along the twisting roads, Clemmie tried hard to remember the old Sperry Stud. She had come north before the parents had; she had answered a Queensland ad and won herself her first job here. It was through some Brisbane newspapers that she had happened to send down that Daryl had decided one chilly grey morning in Melbourne to retire to 'the finest and loveliest realty Australia can offer.' (Amber, having followed her sister to see what she was about, had helped, too, of course.) But Sperry? Clemmie frowned. Sperry at Glen Tally? Ah, yes, she remembered now, she remembered being told that Sperry had been one of the original studs. But that was all she knew.

She wondered if since then Sperry had prospered or receded, worse still if it was at that trying in-between state, neither good nor bad. Mediocrity was always a hard condition to handle. When she found the place, she would park the car some distance away and reconnoitre first. If it was too impossible, too unattractive, she would proceed to her Brisbane flat and ring the man from there, tell him No. Then she grimaced, thinking what a fool she would be, ringing someone whose name she could not decipher. If she had taken the job certainly her first chore would have been to tell him not to obliterate his name by an old property stamp. Clemmie changed gears, for the terrain was becoming steep, and a mountain was about to be crossed.

Why, she frowned, grinding upwards, had the fellow contacted *her*? She had worked very close with Lindsay, but never once, except to say it had been an original, had she heard him mention Sperry.

Meanwhile, and enjoyably, Clemmie found time to look around her, look around Australia's summer country, only a handful of days in a year without a blue sky and a shining sun.

As far as she could see gentle green hills unrolled to the west, lovely untouched hills with no more than three or four white farmlets showing, half-merged into the white trunks of the silver gums that grew up here, sometimes so much a part of the white scene that only a blue thread of woodsmoke marked their separate existence.

Then she saw a cluster of houses that did *not* merge, a brown cluster that meandered untidily over the floor of the foothills, too many buildings and barns for a farmlet, but the size of a—stud?

She descended and approached the brown conglomeration dubiously. After the studs she had attended with Lindsay, the prospect was certainly uninviting. No white fences, no immaculate arrangement, no——

'No!' Clemmie said aloud. 'It's not the background I want, even in my anxious state.'

But before she turned back and went on to Brisbane she had better make sure that this was really the old Sperry Stud. There was a thicket of wild lime some distance off the road, and she drove across and parked

her small car in the middle of it. It concealed it success-
fully, indeed you would have to come right up to it before you saw it. Satisfied, she set off to the brown conglomeration on foot.

There was no one in sight when Clemmie examined
the sagging gate, so she could take her time tracing the
faded letters. Sperry Stud, her fingers found. So this
was the place she was looking for. Looking for but with
no intention of continuing on with, was her instant
judgment. She did not mind a degree of run-downness,
but the property was in definite bad repair. She could
not imagine how she could have been offered a post
here, not, anyway, for a long time yet.

She wandered up to the house itself and peered
through some of the windows; she examined several
barns. At length, having finished the building inspec-
tion, and been progressively discouraged, she decided
to give Sperry its fair chance by giving its surrounding
fields a quick look-over before she went on to Brisbane
and phoned that obliterated name. But, and Clemmie
paused ruefully, realising something for the first time,
how was she to do so, for there might have been a con-
nection once, but there was none now. All the wires
were down.

Shrugging, she set across the knee-deep grass to look
for any signs of stock. She found nothing, yet some
cakes of manure indicated that there was something,
and once she even traced the print of a hoof. A fairly
recent hoofprint. Curiouser and curiouser, Clemmie
smiled.

She walked on, forgetting her disappointment that
the letter she had received yesterday was not to be her
escape after all, that it couldn't be, not with a run-down
place like this, forgetting everything in the loveliness of

the terrain. For the flats, where once horses must have been exercised, were ending in ferny glades, glades punctuated here and there with old, now fern-festooned diggings, and Clemmie knew what these were. Some quite precious 'semi-precious' stones had been dug up here—sapphires, beryls, lesser rubies and diamonds, for this was gem country, and this was how dug terrain was left.

Again Clemmie saw a hoofprint, and stepping between twigs and brambles she followed it up. She saw another fern-festooned digging, quite a large one, and was about to move on when she heard the noise. It was only a small noise, barely a stir, and she would have dismissed it as one of the hundred noises the bush can make had she not noted in the sound a slight whicker—a horse's tired whicker. She had worked with animals too long not to recognise that tone.

She stood very still, waiting for the whicker to repeat itself. It did not, so perhaps she had imagined it, yet there *had* been a print leading here, and she could see no print on the other side of the digging.

She listened again. She listened so intently she hardly drew a breath. Nothing—no whicker, no movement. And yet——

Now she was approaching the digging, bending over it, staring into a dark void. How deep was it down there? Semi-precious stones were usually surface-won, so perhaps this miner had had his eye on gold. Gold! Clemmie stepped forward again, leaned, leaned right over . . . then lost her balance and stumbled. The next moment she was pitching forward into the black hole. How deep a hole she was not to agonise over then, nor was she to wonder at something fiercely threshing as she slid down on top of it.

The threshing continued for some time, then stopped. The morning grew into afternoon, the afternoon marched towards night.

Clemmie, oblivious, still lay there.

When Clemmie opened her eyes and *really* saw, for though she had fluttered her lids many times she had known nothing at all, she was lying in a bed in a room. What bed, what room, she did not know, and it did not need the quiet voice somewhere near her bidding her to take it slowly for her to do just that. She closed her eyes again.

But eventually she wanted to open and keep her eyes open. Her glance went round the room she had never seen before; an ordinary room, she found, containing only basic furniture. The bed in which she lay was clean but certainly basic too.

'Not the Grand Hotel,' the voice that had bade her take it slowly agreed.

Clemmie tried to see the owner of the voice, but her neck was too stiff for her to turn it and the voice owner was out of her eye range. There was something about the voice, though. It was male and it was vaguely familiar. She waited for it to speak again.

'To help you in your confusion, I'll put you in the picture,' the voice obliged her. 'It's morning. The morning after, as far as I can judge, you disappeared down a black hole.'

'Oh, yes, the hole!' she remembered.

'You'd been down there all that day, I estimate, but thank heaven, not all night. I found you around sunset, brought you back here, and—well, that's it.'

'There's quite a lot left out. How did you find me?'

'I recognised the car in the lime thicket.'———

Recognised?——— 'It's only small, but not that small, especially when you were expected.'—Expected?—'I guessed at once that you'd parked it there while you cased the place.'

'Cased it?' she queried.

'Saw if it was any good going on with it. Was it?'

'Saw what was any good?'

'The job I'd written about,' said the voice.

'The—— Who are you?'

'The fellow who wrote offering you the post. I just said so.'

'But—who else?'

'I think,' he said, 'you must be starting to remember my voice.'

'Yes,' Clemmie returned, 'and I'm beginning to piece things together. You just said you recognised Miss Muff——my car.'

'I did.'

'Then *who are you*?' she insisted.

'I'm the same man you kindly put to bed, Miss Green, after an encounter with a bear—sorry, koala—and I'm now returning the courtesy.'

'*You* put me here!' she gasped.

'Just like you put me there.'

'But there's a difference,' Clemmie said frozenly. 'I put you to bed—well, as you were.'

'As I was?' He pretended puzzlement.

'I only took your jacket off, but——'

'But?'

'But that was all.'

'And is that all you're worrying about? What a fuss over a mere pair of pyjamas! Did you want an alluring negligée, then? I was fresh out of those.'

'You put me in——'

'Yes, I put you into my pyjamas,' he nodded. 'Too long, too wide, but at the time——' He had crossed into eye range now and she found herself looking into the amused eyes of Rickaby Roen.

'You!' Although she had guessed it, the realisation still came as a shock.

'Yes,' he smiled.

'You bought old Sperry?' she guessed.

'Yes. Now how about some tuck?' He nodded to a tray he had brought in, and, about to refuse, Clemmie realised she was very hungry and decided to keep any hostilities until later when she was fed and better physically equipped. She allowed him to sit her up, finding herself unable to stop a cry of pain as he did so.

'Yes, you're cut and probably by this time well on the way to some nasty bruising,' he nodded. 'But eat now. You must be starved. We'll see to those injuries again later.'

'Again——?' she said faintly.

'Again,' he said firmly, and handed her a bowl of soup.

She was ravenous, otherwise she would not have accepted the bowl he put in her hands.—Yet would she have had any alternative? She had a strong feeling that this man always got what he wanted, be it the acceptance of a bowl of soup or——

She felt herself flushing, and gave her whole attention to the broth.

'Yes,' he broke in quietly, reading her in some uncanny way, 'I do. I get what I want.'

She drained the soup, and, feeling bolder, stronger, looked up at him.

'Always?'

'To date I have,' he assured her.

'You must have led a charmed life,' she commented.

'No, just a very hard and very determined life. I knew from the start what I wanted, so I worked hard at it.'

'Lots of people do that, but still don't achieve anything.' Clemmie added a little uncertainly, daunted by the cool confidence in the eyes looking into hers: 'I mean in the end.'

'In the end I will,' he assured her. 'Here's the next course.' It was beef stew, tinned probably, but still enticing to someone who had fasted so long. 'While you eat I'll put a few more details in that picture.'

'Thank you.'

'I've purchased Sperry,' he began.

'Yes,' she said. 'I'm surprised. You don't seem the animal sort.'

'I'm not, but I'll be in anything I can see a possible return from, be it real estate, koalas' ... a pause ... 'girls.'

'Oh, you buy girls?' Clemmie made her voice light and supremely uninterested. It was hard. She was very interested.

'Change that girls,' he said. 'Just now I'm only interested in one.'

'For a possible return?'

'Yes.'

A silence, a rather uncomfortable one.

'I hear you coaxed Fitzroy's share in Summer Heights away from him.' Clemmie broke the silence.

'A sufficient number of dollars eliminates any need for coaxing.'

'I don't think Mr Osborne will be so easy,' she told him. 'He's been in the project as long as Mr Malling, so there'll be a degree of sentiment to overcome there.'

'So he'll require more money,' Rickaby Roen shrugged. 'No worry.'

'You think you can buy anything, don't you?' she said curiously.

'Most people have their price,' he shrugged.

'Most—but not all?'

'So near to all it won't matter. This time next year, of the firm of Malling, Fitzroy and Osborne there won't even be a Malling.'

'But there will be a Roen?' she asked demeaningly.

'A Roen,' he answered blandly.

'I think you're in for a shock,' Clemmie smiled; she tried to smile patronisingly.

'I know, not think, *you* are. All right, we'll leave that and come to Sperry. As you see, now I've bought out Sperry.'

'At a bargain price, I sincerely hope. The stud is in near decay.'

'The old man stood out for his price. In the end I gave it to him.'

'You were a fool,' she said.

'No. I knew it would return what I wanted returned.'

'But how can it? It's in serious disrepair. On your own admission you know nothing of the world of horses——'

'Or dogs, cats, wombats,' he tacked on. 'But you didn't listen to me. I said: "I knew it would return what I wanted returned."'

'Yes, I heard you.'

'But didn't follow, I think. What I *wanted* returned, were my words.'

'Look, Mr Roen——' she began.

'Rickaby.'

'Look, Mr Roen, I believe you've been unwise in your purchase.'

'No—wise,' he contradicted. 'In fact it was the only way to go about things.'

'What things?' she asked.

'To be brief—you.'

'Me?' she queried.

'You. A little matter of a marriage proposal.'

'A marriage proposal? Oh, you want Amber after all, and you need me to help you pull it off, so you've got me here to——'

'Lord no! I don't want her, never did. I want you. I could have done it through the expected channels, that is present myself at your stepfather's house, all that, but that would be as distasteful to him as it would be to me. This way he can give his blessing without a qualm.'

'My stepfather would always have a qualm,' Clemmie said in an unreal voice. She could not believe what she had heard. 'He would have considerable qualms about your money going to me and not to Amber.' She added hastily: 'Had it happened, but it won't.'

'It will, but I agree with you that he would have qualms, as you put it. On the other hand, he would be glad to have you off his hands. The little you've told me of your stepfather has assured me that he would accept me with his ears back.'

'Accept Rickaby Roen?' broke in Clemmie with laughter. 'Accept Amber's——well, Amber's——'

'*Non*-lover. Yes.'

'You're mad!' she gasped.

'Oh, no. The Coyles, on your own admission the other night, are now in the throes of joining your sister and young Malling in holy matrimony. Right?'

'No—yes—I mean——'

'Right, then. So they naturally don't want you about.'

'Why wouldn't they?' she demanded.

'Because, you little blind idiot, you'd upset the applecart, because you're too damn lovely—yes, I'm saying that. You're far too good a thing to have around at the same time as the other.'

'As Amber?' she said sarcastically. 'Now I *know* you're mad!'

'I'm certainly not. And young Malling will know that, too, once the smoke gets out of his eyes and he sees clearly again. But until it does, action, Coyle-action, must take place and take place fast. If the action means Rickaby Roen for you, then curses but relief at the same time.'

Clemmie was looking at him incredulously. 'Quite mad,' she judged again. 'Why, you're talking almost as though——'

'As though I'm going to marry you? Then it's not mad talk. It's true.'

'But you don't even know me,' she gasped.

'I didn't know the first project I bought in Western Australia ten years ago, but I sensed it would be all right, and it was. I didn't know with any of the others later.'

'But I'm not a project.'

He shrugged. 'I can still sense things, sense them intrinsically, and it comes out you. It's as simple and as basic as that.'

'It isn't simple, it's outrageous!'

'Sweets,' he returned calmly, and handed over a dish of pears and cream.

She ate mutinously, not speaking. Her silence did

not seem to worry him, he sat waiting for her to be done.

'When you're finished,' he told her, 'we'll do those wounds again.'

'We won't,' she contradicted. 'I'm all right.'

'They'll still be attended to.'

'Then I'll do them myself.'

'Not thoroughly. You'd have to be double-jointed. Are you finished yet?'

'As finished as I'll ever be, Mr Roen, because——'

Clemmie did not finish herself. The tray was taken from her. From somewhere a bowl of hot water was produced, soap, sponge, towel, then, quite airily, bed-clothes were drawn down.

'Turn over,' he said.

'I won't!' she burst out.

'A bit difficult then, because over is where your damage is, that's how you landed.'

'I won't!'

'In which case——' Calmly he leaned across and turned Clemmie to the mattress.

Ten minutes later she was sitting up again, distinctly more comfortable in herself, and——

And despising Rickaby Roen to the end of the earth.

Still, she had to know things, and sulking would avail her nothing. She decided not to mention those pre-posterous, ridiculous ideas he had tossed at her regarding marriage and his intrinsic knowledge of knowing the end result, so she skipped them and concentrated on his purchase of Sperry.

'I can't believe it was just because of me' ... she flushed and altered that to 'my ability' ... 'that you purchased something you know nothing at all about.'

'You'd be right. I'm always, of course, first and fore-most a business man.'

'Of course,' sarcastically.

'I knew that this hinterland had some of Australia's finest studs. I'd never dabbled in horseflesh, and the idea attracted me, especially when I learned there was a run-down place on the market. I felt a challenge, a challenge I had to accept ... particularly when any staff trouble was pre-solved.'

'How do you mean?'

'You,' he said.

'How did you know I'd accept? I haven't now.'

'I didn't know, I still don't, but I think you will. You see, I saw your eyes that evening when you looked at a bear ... koala ... looked at him for injury.'

'Well?'

'You had deep feeling there,' he explained. 'I can't pretend to follow it, I've always been a figures, not a creature man. But love was certainly there.'

'Well?'

'I knew you would love here, love the few poor specimens that came with my purchase. I knew you would love to tend them.'

'There are other places with the same work,' she shrugged.

'You really mean without me.'

She did not deny that. She said: 'For all you really know I'm quite incapable.'

'Oh, no, I traced your ex-boss's new location in Sydney and contacted him. He gave a glowing report.'

'You contacted Lindsay?' she said.

'Yes.'

'And then you bought Sperry?'

'Yes.'

'You must have money to waste,' she said dryly.

'Money, but not to waste.'

'This was waste,' Clemmie insisted.

'Not the way I see it.'

'It will take years to do anything.'

'What I'm after will only take a month.'

She stared at him. 'Mad!' she said again.

'I was not,' he smiled, 'talking about the stud.'

'Anyway,' Clemmie went on hurriedly, 'you've done it, so it's no use holding post-mortems.'

'I'm holding no post-mortems, I'm looking ahead.'

'To a Melbourne Cup winner,' she said scornfully.

'No, to us.'

'I won't be here,' she insisted.

'Oh, yes, you will.'

She mulled that over for a furious minute. Then:

'As soon as you leave this room, Mr Roen, I'm getting up,' she announced.

'Why wait till then? You weren't so pernickety before.'

'I was unconscious before. You didn't tell me what happened after you noticed the car and concluded that I was—casing the place.'

'I looked around for you,' he said. 'I shudder now to think what the result would have been had I not seen the hoofprints.'

'Yes, I saw them, too. I followed them. Did you find the horse? The marks stopped where I did.'

'Exactly, and I found him where I found you, and that was on top of him, fortunately. If it had been the other way about I might as well have sealed up the digging there and then.'

'Was it that? A digging?' she asked.

'An old gold bid. Someone on the look-out for semi-precious stones must have believed they saw a sign of gold, and really got to work with a pick.'

'Yes, it went a fair way down,' she agreed.

'You can say that. Getting you out nearly killed me.'

'But you did it,' Clemmie pointed out.

'You're here,' he grinned. 'Fortunately you were out to it. The last thing I wanted was maidenly squeals as to how you were brought up.'

Clemmie flushed.

'Then you carried me to the house,' she said, 'and——'

'Yes,' he nodded, 'and——'

'Couldn't you have got a neighbour to come along? —Some neighbour's *wife*?'

'None for miles, and anyway, it couldn't wait. Besides, you woke up comfortable enough, didn't you? What are you complaining about?'

'You,' she said bitterly. 'The very least you could have done was fetch a doctor.'

'Doctors are far-away guys out here. Also, you were not hurt, only jarred, bruised, but nothing amiss.'

'How would you know?'

'The usual way, of course.' He grinned impudently at her. 'I found out for myself. I cleaned you up—you were filthy. I rugged you up. Then I went out to see what could be done about the other fellow.'

'The other fellow? You mean the pony I landed on? But how did he get there?'

'The same way as you, no doubt. He would miss his footing. He would be leaning over for some succulent titbit ... the grass is always greener on the other side ... and down he would go.'

'Had he been there long?' she asked.

'He couldn't tell me,' Rickaby Roen replied.

'You know what I mean. Was he ... is he ...'

'Well, how would you be with four legs, not two, trying to fit into a deep narrow hole like that? How would you like to have a body suddenly descend on you?'

'Did I injure him?' she asked anxiously.

'I don't think you did him any good.' A shrug. 'But don't worry, because I'm not worrying any more.'

'Why? What do you mean by that?'

'An injured horse, I've been told, is a liability. Liabilities are things I've never allowed in my working life.'

'You mean you——' Clemmie stared at Rickaby Roen in horror and disbelief.

'Yes, I mean that,' he nodded.

'You mean you would—destroy him?'

'How do you know I haven't already?'

'I don't know,' Clemmie said piteously. 'Have you?'

'With you around my neck, where could I have found the time?'

'Then you haven't. And you mustn't, of course.'

'No, "of course". I seriously intend Sperry to become a prize stud, and in a prize stud there's no room for crocks.'

'But he needn't be a crock. He might still be able to be mended—nursed—attended to.'

'Very touching, but that's not what I had in mind for here.'

'Please can I at least see him?' she begged.

'But you're not staying on, are you—your own words—so why bother? No, it would be better if you didn't see him. If you're the sentimental sort you could even carry a distasteful picture away with you. You

could persuade yourself in the end that you even caused
his death. Hi, what are you doing?'

For Clemmie was getting up, painfully, but barely
conscious of the pain, not caring that the over-big
pyjama suit he had put on her was falling away in
several places since there was too little of her to stop it,
only anxious to get out and see ... and save.

He let her go.

But had Clemmie turned round she would have seen
him smiling to himself, a triumphant smile.

'He's in the lean-to,' he called out, 'that's as far as
I could carry him.'

Clemmie stopped. 'You carried a——'

'Small pony. Yes, he's small pony size, otherwise the
shaft would still be full of horse. I couldn't have shifted
anything larger. Now' ... catching up with Clemmie
and walking with her, as unconscious of the comical
spectacle she made in his pyjamas as Clemmie was ...
'you'll see how landing, as you did, was such a disaster.
Oh, yes, he'll certainly have to be put down.'

'Only over my dead body.' Clemmie was running
now, one hand keeping up the pyjama pants that kept
wriggling over her hips.

'Which you will have at any moment, exposing
yourself like that. It may be endless summer up here,
but——'

With that he caught her to him, tied the pyjama cord
securely, then picked her up under his arm and carried
her the rest of the way to where he had deposited the
pony. Thankful for his consideration in not hurting the
wounds she had gathered for herself in that carrying,
Clemmie remembered *how* he knew about the wounds,
and bit her lip. He knew where not to touch, she

thought, and she would have slid herself to the ground, except that the hands, ostensibly casual, were iron-hard around her now, and she was forced to remain where she was.

But when they reached the old lean-to, he put her down, steadied her a moment so she could regain her balance, then nodded to the floor.

'I don't think even a bullet is called for,' he said, 'the feller is nearly gone.'

Clemmie did not answer him. She was kneeling on the ground, touching, feeling, probing the poor little battered creature. She was not aware that tears were streaming down her cheeks.

'Don't cry,' Roen advised. 'I'll put him out of his misery.' Clemmie heard him walk off.

'No!' she said to herself. She also said it to the small thing, though it was beyond hearing, she knew that.

'No. No!' she cried to Rickaby Roen now, for he had come back.

'Can you make it to the homestead on your own?' he asked.

'I'm not leaving.'

'You can't stay here and watch.'

'I'm staying,' she insisted.

'Look, I promise you I'll do it humanely.'

'I'm staying. *I'm staying here, at Sperry, at Glen Tally*—I believe that's what you want. But only if you let me work on her ... by the way, she's a girl and not a feller ... otherwise I'm off at once.'

'That's blackmail,' he said.

'Call it what you like!' snapped Clemmie.

'It's also inhumane. The feller—the girl is beyond repair.'

'Who says so?' she demanded.

'I do, and after all, I'm only a little less knowledge-able than you, you're not a graduated vet.'

'I don't need graduation to bring back that filly.'

'To what? To the state of stud crock. I want no crocks around.'

'Nor me around the place, either, it seems. All right' ... as Clemmie rose ... 'go ahead.'

'As you will?'

'Right ahead to Brisbane. And at once.'

'Well, it seems you win.' He stepped back, put down the rifle. 'If I promise to do nothing will you promise to go back to the house?'

'Yes.'

'Get into bed?'

'No—Oh, all right, yes.'

'Then off you go. And mind those pyjama pants.'

Clemmie hauled them up, re-tied them. 'You won't——'

He sighed. 'I won't. I said so.'

He watched her leave, and as before he smiled to himself, a triumphant smile. He picked up the rifle and squinted down the barrel, checked it, handled it. It was quite a safe thing to do when it was unloaded.

CHAPTER FOUR

CLEMMIE was in bed when Rickaby Roen returned, not out of obedience but from sheer exhaustion. She had had no intention of doing what she had promised him she would, going to her cot like a good little girl and resting there a prescribed time, she had intended instead to come back here to the house and search around the medical cabinet ... there must be some sort of medical cabinet ... and put out any supplies that might help that poor little thing in the lean-to. But pain and weariness had caught up with her, and she had climbed into the crib, only a roll of cottonwool and a bandage to show her concern.

Rickaby must have noticed these items, but he did not comment.

'A vet will be out this afternoon,' he tossed at her.

'How do you know? There's no phone—at least I couldn't see any.'

'I stopped a motorist ... oh, yes, some do pass ... and gave him a message.'

'Then you mean you hope a vet will be along this afternoon?'

'No,' said Roen, 'he will be.'

'I see.' Clemmie did see, she saw the supreme, arrogant confidence of this man.

'What about now?' she asked presently.

'I've covered the young 'un up, covered, also, the exposed end of the lean-to.'

As Clemmie still looked worried, the man asked impatiently: 'What else, then? Did you want her here beside you in bed?'

'It's the vet I'm thinking about,' she explained. 'Are you going to approach him when ... if ... he comes from a business or a personal angle?'

'What do you mean?'

'Some vets will only advise what's expected of them. Oh, they don't lie—they have ethics. After all, they're doctors. But if a client obviously doesn't want to try any more, they'll go along with that.'

'Perfectly legitimate, surely, if the injuries warrant it?' he said.

'But if,' continued Clemmie, 'they see you want to save a life, must save it, they'll go along with that as well. It's really' ... a tentative pause ... 'up to the client.'

'... And the client's employee.'

'If you're looking at me——' she began.

'I am,' he assured her.

'Then I'm not.'

'Not my employee?'

'No.'

'Then thank you at least for telling me. Having achieved your immediate purpose, it seems, you're bowing out after all. Well, I'll know what to tell the doc when he comes.'

'You wouldn't!' she gasped.

'No, Miss Green?'

Clemmie was silent a moment.

'I can't stop here,' she said unhappily at length, 'and that filly will need day *plus* night attention for some time. I mightn't be qualified, but I know that.'

'No worries, then. I'll do the nights, you the days.'

She sighed. 'Mr Roen, please listen to me. I'm

thankful that you've spared the filly, and in return I would be happy to accept the post ... living out as offered in your letter ... but——'

'But?' he queried.

'But still no.'

'What's wrong with you? I just said I'd do the nights if that's the concern. You could drive back to that virtuous couch of yours every evening and commute here just for the day sessions.'

'But,' broke in Clemmie, 'for a week at least, and believe me, the vet will tell you likewise, during your nights you'll need someone extra on hand, someone else in reach, someone with—well, a little more know-how on the subject than you have.'

'You?' he asked.

'Yes.'

'Then——?'

'I can't do it,' she protested. 'I can't live out here just with you.'

'After last night?' he insinuated.

'Especially after last night. What are you staring at?'

'You,' he said. 'I simply can't believe it—not in this age.'

'Well, you'd better start to believe,' she said crossly.

'My dear girl, after last night——'

'Quoting that again only strengthens my case. I was unconscious then, but I'm very conscious now, and, in this age or not, I'm not staying in a house with you.'

He grinned. 'Good lord, the birds and the guys do nothing else these times!'

'Not in the times in which I move,' Clemmie said firmly.

'I think I'm beginning to follow you,' he said. 'I think you're being very aware of your step-parents.'

'Stepfather. My mother is my own mother.'

'You're being very aware of them.'

'Not deliberately,' admitted Clemmie unwillingly, 'but an awareness *is* there, an awareness actually of Amber—I mean, for my sister—as regards Summer Heights.'

'You really mean as regards the Mallings, I think. Oh, yes, I know something about the Mallings as well as son Bruce being our particular Malling in Malling, Osborne and now' ... he smiled ... 'Roen. I know they're upper crust, an upper crust whose standards wouldn't include any of this.' He spread his hands significantly around the room with Clemmie still sitting up in the bed. 'But,' not giving her a chance to speak, 'I'm still not deceived. It's not Amber you're really thinking of, it's Clementine Green. You want no blot on your copybook when the smoke in young Malling's eyes finally clears away and he seeks out his first love again.' A pause. 'Too late.'

Clemmie looked at him in horror.

'You know it's not too late!'

'Do I?' he grinned impudently. 'How would you know, you weren't there to know. Not there in your full senses, I mean. But' ... grinning again at the anger that was robbing her of her voice ... 'that "too late" didn't happen to refer to morals, it referred to Malling's run for you. Too late. You see, I got there first.'

'You—you——' she stammered.

'Yes, you said all that before. Now what do you fancy for lunch?'

'I've just eaten.'

'That was breakfast. I'd prefer to get lunch over before the vet arrives.'

'If he arrives,' she corrected.

'Before he arrives. Incidentally, did you want me to bring him in here, or would you prefer me to relay his instructions?'

'Of course I don't want him brought in here,' she said angrily.

'Then I'll write down the gen and give it to you afterwards. Not that I think that's really wise. A closed door is always a tantalising door to my way of thinking. He could wonder.'

'Wonder what?'

'Oh, come, Miss Green.' Another impudent grin.

'You're preposterous!' she snapped. 'Anyway, he won't wonder, because you'll be asking no instructions for me. I won't be staying.'

'Then neither will the filly.'

She looked at him piteously, and he must have relented a little, for he said: 'You could be wrong, you know, the young 'un might not be as bad as you think, I might be able to get over the dangerous first week alone.'

'But I don't think so,' Clemmie sighed.

The vet, who arrived in the late afternoon ... what gift apart from the making of money did this man possess to bring a busy specialist out this far? ... said precisely the same.

'Intensive care.' Clemmie heard him from the other side of the door. 'There's no break, no rupture, but the filly has had a hell of a shock that could still be fatal. It all depends on her make-up—a phlegmatic beast could shake it off, a nervous one go under. Just like humans really. You said you had someone with some experience out here?'

'Yes. A very good hand,' said Rickaby Roen.

'Then he'll know. I'll leave these pills. Your very

good hand will understand all about administering them. Do you want me to have a word with him?'

'He's not here just at present, but as you said, he'll understand.' The last few words were indistinct, so Clemmie knew that Rickaby was conducting the vet out. She looked around for the clothes she had worn yesterday, but could not find them. She wanted to find them, she wanted to dress and hurry out to see what the vet had left for the filly. She was still searching when Roen came back into the house.

'Where are my——' she began.

'On the line,' he forestalled her. 'I washed them.'

'You what?'

'You couldn't have worn them as they were,' he explained calmly, 'they were caked with mud.'

'I want to see the filly's pills.'

'No one is stopping you.'

'I want to be dressed, not——' She saw him open his hateful mouth obviously to say she was not now undressed, and firmed her lips. 'I want my things.'

'It will be done.' He turned and went out to the line. When he came back he tossed the garments through to her and Clemmie closed the door.

She came out soon after and armed with the pills the vet had left they both went down to the lean-to.

Rickaby Roen had made a very good job of enclosing the exposed end of the erection, and when they went inside to the patient, Clemmie saw that he had also made a good job there. The battered little thing was very comfortably ensconced on pillows and protected from any chill that might rise, even in this warm climate, by several fleecy rugs.

'You've made her very snug,' Clemmie said grudgingly. Before Rickaby could begin to bask in her praise, she asked briskly: 'What did the vet say?'

'I told you, and no doubt you also eavesdropped. There's no break, no rupture, but shock. Oh, and the inevitable bruises and abrasions, of course.'

'He didn't suggest taking her into his surgery?'

'As a matter of fact he spoke against it. The important thing, he emphasised, was rest, as little movement as possible. That was why he was pleased with my arrangement.' Rickaby nodded like a proud schoolboy to the improvised ward.

'Did he anticipate any trouble?' she asked.

'Yes,' Rickaby admitted, 'he said we could have some of that for a while.'

'Apart from the rest, the pills, what else?'

'Close vigil.'

'Just as I told you?'

'Just as you told me. What are you doing?' For Clemmie was squatting down beside the little filly and unstoppering bottles.

'Close vigil,' she tossed back. 'It has to start somewhere.' She picked up the pills. She knew she was good at this. Lindsay had always called upon her for his pill pushing.

'You're staying, Clemmie!'

'Pass me that sponge.'

When Clemmie rose again the small animal had fallen into a serene slumber, one that with luck might last some hours.

'What are you going to call her?' Clemmie asked as they returned to the house.

'Not having any big stakes in mind for the brat, I doubt if it matters,' he said. 'The brown filly will be all she'll probably get.'

'Except that she's very clearly going to be chestnut. Also, of course it matters. She's a thing, a breathing, pulsing——'

'A very thready pulse just now.'

'—animal,' ignored Clemmie, 'and she can't be called just "she" or "it" or "her" or "the brown filly".'

'Would you care to name she, it, her, the brown filly, then?' he invited.

'She's yours, not mine.'

'Well, then she's Clematis. There's one Clementine already, so now we'll have the flower version of it.'

'You must know other names,' she protested.

'No.'

'Of course you do. Your sister's.'

'No sister. And no mother, cousin, aunt. I only know Clementine.'

'But you must have had girls,' she persisted.

'Only you, Clemmie.'

'I'm not, and anyway, I don't believe you. At the very least you know Amber.'

'That's a stone,' he corrected.

'Also a colour.' To her embarrassment and dismay Clemmie heard herself asking him: 'What colour, Mr Roen?'

'For Amber?'

'Yes.'

'Golden. Golden Amber.'

'Then what colour am I?'

She felt his big arm suddenly stopping her, turning her round to estimate her. She saw his eyes meet her own blue eyes. His were very dark, but still with that reddish gleam.

'You're young leaf green,' he said. 'You're the

colour that comes after the budding but before the
fruit. You're the finish of spring yet the beginning of
summer. You are——'

'And you're not the business man that you think,
you're a poet.' Clemmie spoke a little breathlessly.
She disengaged herself and they finished the walk to
the house.

There she rummaged round an extremely basic
kitchen and managed to produce a passable meal.

'It's not very elaborate,' she apologised as she put
down a plain omelette; she had managed to find eggs
and milk and a pan in which to cook them, but when
it had come to a variation and a garnish, she had
found nothing in the galley to help her.

'It's excellent,' Rickaby appreciated. 'Where did
you learn to be a Cordon Bleu cook?'

'I'm not,' she contradicted, 'what I can produce
most eldest in the family are expected to.'

'I was an eldest child,' he argued.

'Then you didn't just grow? You said' ... in explanation ... 'you had no mother, cousin, aunt.'

'I must have had a mother, mustn't I?' he
shrugged.

'You didn't know her? Then how did you know
you were the eldest?'

'Eldest, in between and youngest—that's mostly
the pattern in orphanages. I was at several homes and
I only encountered non-loners once.'

'You were brought up in a home?' she queried.

'I said several homes. Different age groups, you
see.'

'I'm sorry,' Clemmie said quietly.

'Oh, they were all good,' Rickaby assured her.

'So you have no regrets?'

'Oh, yes, I have regrets. If I hadn't, I wouldn't be working towards what I am now.'

'And what's that?'

'A happy fambly. We used to play Happy Famblies in the homes—we called it that. I even believed that was its correct name until I was quite big.'

'And then?' Clemmie said a little hurriedly. He had his eyes on her again, his dark eyes with the red gleams, and though she tried to look away she had to look back again.

'And then I reached the age of looking after myself, so with that happy fambly still in view I made my first forward bid. Do you want to hear about it?'

'If it ends in dollars——'

'It does.'

'Then it doesn't matter. Didn't you have any failures?' she asked in distaste.

'Not one. That's why I can't visualise failure this time.'

'You mean in your purchase of the stud?'

'Stud?' He looked uncomprehending for a moment.

'Sperry,' she explained.

'Oh, Sperry. I was thinking of something else.'

Clemmie got up and poured coffee. She thought it was time she changed the subject.

'Have you examined your purchase yet?' she asked. 'I mean, gone over it properly.?'

'Not from a specialist's angle. Shall we drink this and then go and inspect?'

'I'm no specialist,' she said again.

'But you would know what's required.'

'Yes, I would know that.'

'Then let's begin at once.' He drained his drink

and banged the mug down. Clemmie put hers down, and they walked together out of the house.

'The homestead will have to be fixed up,' Rickaby nodded as they proceeded, 'it's pretty primitive in parts.'

'Don't add too much,' appealed Clemmie, for she quite liked its old colonial look.

But once out in Sperry's surrounding fields, Clemmie added quite a lot, for animal backgrounds, be they studs, kennels or catteries, were her best-loved chores.

She told Rickaby where he should put his foaling boxes, how a sitter's quarters should be handy, how all doors should open outward and fasten back, allow an abundance of light and a source of fresh air, how a sand roll must be included, several varying exercise rings. She even got on to kitchens for special diets, a swimming pool exclusively for horses, a——

'Hold hard,' he interrupted, 'you're getting me in too deep!'

'A horse pool has to be deep.'

'You know I didn't mean that, you know I meant money.'

'Of which you have a lot. Besides, Melbourne Cup winners require money.'

He grinned at that. 'There's none of that sort here, I'd say, no Melbourne Cup winners.'

'Apart from Clematis, as you've called her, is there any stock of any sort?' Clemmie was looking around.

'According to the inventory I received with my receipt there are two stallions and two mares some-where in the outer paddocks. I'm hoping from that number to build a bigger number. Perhaps' ... hope-fully ... 'there's a bigger number even now.'

'Don't be silly,' said Clemmie, 'it's not the right time.'

'You mean not all the time is the right time?' he asked.

'You know very little, don't you?'

'Will you teach me?'

Clemmie set her lips and turned in the direction of the outer paddocks. 'We may as well see them.'

'You didn't answer my question.'

For reply Clemmie strode ahead.

The four, when found, were grassing, and took little notice of them when they came up to the fence.

'Any promises among them?' Rickaby asked after Clemmie had taken a long look.

'If I say no does that mean you'll be thinking of ways to rid yourself of them?'

'Don't make me too detestable, Clemmie, these guys and girls are not in pain like poor Clematis was. I was only thinking of her.'

'Then they're safe, I guess,' accepted Clemmie. 'No, no promises, but a polo club might be interested in those two, possibly a pony club in the others.'

'Thank you.' A pause. 'You never told me when *they* were interested in *each other*.'

'I'll get you a book,' Clemmie promised, and proceeded back to the house.

When she arrived there it was to a large box of groceries placed on the table. She could see that as well as cans and bottles there were packages of frozen vegetables and meat.

'A good fairy has been,' she called.

'It would be the telephone bloke,' Rickaby told her.

'Telephone?'

'I sent another message per passing motorist this

morning asking for re-connection, then suggesting a food hamper on account at the same time.'

... You would, thought Clemmie. Aloud she recalled: 'There were no wires.'

'If you look out you'll see there are now, luckily the essentials were still intact. So here we are, not only in touch but well stocked.'

'And I can ring,' Clemmie appreciated.

'I rather hoped you would say "And I can cook a decent meal".'

'I will. But it's nice not to feel isolated.'

'I don't agree.'

'Perhaps you've always been a loner,' she suggested.

'In an orphanage!'

'Then a wishful loner.'

'Nor that, either, though I admit I never fancied a crowd. I always dreamed of being one of a twosome. Still do.'

'It must have been all those Happy Famblies.' Before he could disagree, Clemmie asked: 'Chops or steak?'

At eight o'clock the two of them went down to see Clematis again, and the invalid was doing well.

'But you'll still——' prompted Clemmie.

'I'll still watch,' he promised, 'though she seems right enough to me.'

'And you will,' Clemmie went on, 'call me.'

'No, I'm taking over the entire night shift, I told you.'

'I meant if anything doesn't seem right.'

'I'll call,' he assured her. 'Now if I were you I'd have an early night. You've recovered quicker than

Clematis, Clemmie, but you're still not on top, and I
might need you there.'

'Yes,' Clemmie agreed, and went off.

She wondered as she climbed into the cot whether
she should have rung her parents, told them where
she was. But while she was wondering, weighing up
the possibility of her mother asking her who actually
owned Sperry and then becoming silent when she was
told, Clemmie fell asleep, a lighter sleep than last
night, a sleep Rickaby Roen broke into very easily
around midnight, in fact he only put his hand on
Clemmie's arm.

'Clemmie!' he whispered.

'What is it?' Clemmie was already sitting up. 'The
filly?'

'Yes. I hate disturbing you, but I know how you'll
be in the morning if—— Hi, she's not dead yet!'
For Clemmie was pulling jeans over pyjama trousers,
tucking a pyjama top into the pants. Because the
pyjamas were far too big for this tucking, she knew
she must look like a round ball.

'Torch?' she asked.

'Here. And two lanterns are lit at the lean-to. What
are you doing?' For Clemmie was taking rugs off her
bed.

'She has to be kept warm if it's reaction, and it
must be that.'

'She's well rugged now. Anyway, you can't do
that, they're all I have here, and you'll be cold when
you get back into bed.'

'Oh, no, I won't be.' Clemmie spoke with pre-
knowledge.

'You mean you'll be sharing my bed,' he deliberately misunderstood. 'You didn't tell me you cared.'

'This isn't a time for joking,' she said crossly.

'I wasn't joking.'

'Rickaby, for heaven's sake!' Clemmie stopped. Why, she thought, I called him Rickaby. 'I really meant when I said that that I don't think I'll be coming back here tonight.' She nodded for him to light the way across to the lean-to, and they started down.

Halfway there the torchlight was not needed, the lantern beams took over. They lit up the shivering little filly.

Clemmie put over the rugs she had brought, took a good look, then bade Rickaby go back to the house and bring his own rugs, bring everything he could lay his hands on, towels, drapes, tablecloths, even mats.

'But——' he began.

'And *hurry*!'

After he had gone she squatted beside the sick animal. There was little she could do, she was wretchedly aware of that, save stroke, smooth, soothe, reassure and replace rugs as they were kicked off. The filly had had her pills, and until the next dose the rest was up to her, with, of course, her attendant's encouragement. Clemmie fervently encouraged now, aware that Rickaby had returned with his bundle of warmth.

They sat by the filly. Sometimes the little thing threshed, sometimes she shivered, sometimes she lay deathly still. It was during a deathly stillness, the only movement the filly's seeking, asking, begging, flicking brown eyes, that Clemmie said desperately: 'She's terribly, terribly ill. Oh, my darling, do get better, because I love you, do you hear me? I want you to live because I love you.' Without turning to

Rickaby she directed: 'Tell her you love her, too.'

'I love you,' Rickaby complied, but his eyes were on Clemmie. She felt rather than saw the direction, and ordered: 'Tell *her*.'

'Clematis, get better.' Rickaby put out his hand and stroked, as Clemmie was stroking.

'Does this mumbo-jumbo ever work?' he asked presently.

'It helps,' she assured him. 'I've seen a gentle word and a kind hand pull a dog through a crisis, I've watched Lindsay perform the miracle. Then once we had a kitten——'

'But something like this?' Rickaby looked down at the stricken filly.

'There's a saying in horse lore,' Clemmie told him to break the tension, 'that love is eight cold nights in a paddock. A birth can take that long.'

'Well, this is the result of a digging and not love,' said Rickaby practically, 'and I can tell you right now it's not going to grow into eight, not for us.'

He was right. It didn't. It grew into ten. What they did that night, they did for nine more nights, and at times a depleted Clemmie wondered pitifully if she had been wise and humane preventing Rickaby from putting the little thing out of her distress on that first day.

Even though, for endurance's sake, they worked out a sensible roster, three hours on for each of them, the burden was devastating. On the last day, when the change for the better in Clematis was so visible, so definite, that they knew the crisis was over, they were near-robots. Like robots they moved automatically back to the house, spoke mechanically, drank, ate, leaned back and shut burning eyes.

'There's a pile of newspapers on the verandah,' Clemmie said thickly.

'They started to accumulate the morning after That Night.' That Night was the night the filly had decided life was not worth living, and had almost been hauled back from death by them.

'Unopened.' Clemmie barely mouthed it.

'Yes.'

'Funny to think the world has still been going on.'

'I expect that the world would say the same about us—Clemmie! Clemmie?'

For Clemmie was staring at the paper she had plucked idly from the heap, a Brisbane paper. What she was reading she had expected, but she had not expected it so soon, she had not thought ...

'What is it, Clemmie?' Rickaby was asking with concern. 'Don't do the Clematis act on me, I couldn't cope. Ten cold nights in a paddock is enough, my girl. I can't face any more.'

Clemmie handed the paper over. She tried to find words, flippant, brittle words, but they eluded her. Perhaps it was reaction from the last week making her hollow and empty and depleted like this, she did not know, she only knew she had never felt so bruised, so aching in all her life. She had anticipated what would happen with Amber and Bruce, but she had not thought it would happen so soon, and bring such pain.

'Mr and Mrs Daryl Coyle of Summer Heights Estate announce with pleasure the engagement of their younger daughter Amber to Bruce Malling of Melbourne, and also of Summer Heights Estate.'

Rickaby put down the paper to look across at Clemmie, but Clemmie had slipped out of the room.

CHAPTER FIVE

How long for a dream to die?

That was what Clemmie was asking herself as she raced across the Sperry fields away from the old house.

She had known all along what would happen, when Amber came it inevitably happened. It had happened at high school, it had happened at every date Clemmie had had since then. Amber, though three years younger, had dazzled ... mesmerised could have been the word ... with her poise, sophistication and superb looks. On top of that, Clemmie admitted too late, she had not helped things by leaving those two to each other. Oh, yes, she had aided and abetted it, and she had known the certain end, but still a foolish dream had persisted, and now the dream was dying. How long till death?

She wanted it dead, she wanted it all over, all finished, she wanted to forget Bruce and what he had almost come to mean to her. Almost. Her eager mind pounced on that word. Keep to that *almost*, she urged herself. You didn't quite make it with Bruce, perhaps he didn't with you, perhaps it was only ever almost for both of you. Almost. Almost. Clemmie was not aware that she was crying brokenly aloud.

The sun ... Clemmie realised in numb surprise that it must already be late afternoon from the length of the golden beams ... was lighting up the red tips of the tops of the eucalypt trees. Only yesterday she had noticed the same shining exhibition, and it had lit her heart, lit it in spite of a sick filly. But now, totally unlit, she did not see the fields, the grazing stock that Rickaby had acquired with his purchase of Sperry, she saw the Summer Heights Estate instead.

She was back there for a week-end from her Brisbane flat, and she was looking up the rise to the Coyles' nearest neighbour in this new exclusive promotion.

'He's one of the company directors,' her mother had nodded, following her daughter's glance, and Clemmie had understood that Alison had meant someone in the house and not the house itself as it absurdly sounded.

'Rolling in money, no doubt,' Clemmie had tossed flippantly; she had always talked like that to the family, they had expected it.

'I wouldn't know, Clementine' ... reprovingly and probably untruly ... 'but I'm sure with a new home like that——' A pause, a long and significant pause, Clemmie recalled, and then:

'For your own sake, and ours, please don't shrug your shoulders and pass this chance over. Opportunities like Mr Malling don't drop out of trees.'

'What do you mean, Mother?'

'Mr Bruce Malling—one of the partners, and in this instance the partner who owns that home. It would be very satisfactory to us if you—if he—— Not such a match as it seems Amber will have in her Mr Roen, but——'

'But in my circumstances quite a windfall, you mean?'

'Really, Clementine!' Alison had said, shocked.

'Have you met him?' Clemmie had asked ... after she had counted a silent ten.

'I've seen and heard of him.'

'Old, I suppose.'

'Young,' said her mother.

'Married?'

'Clementine, as though I would be talking like this if he were!'

'What's an unmarried young man doing in such a big house?' asked Clemmie.

'I wouldn't dream of asking, and I trust you won't, either. I hope the two of you meet, find much in common, and—— Well, after all, Clementine, as Daryl was saying——'

Clemmie had known what her stepfather had been saying, he had always made it quite plain to Clemmie that he did not want his later years intruded upon. *But*, Clemmie remembered, he had never said it to Amber, not to her knowledge.

'So I'm to try my wiles on this boy wonder, am I, Mother?' Again the brittleness that had been expected of her had been produced.

'Really, Clementine——'

'Don't worry, dear.' Clemmie had wandered away. Don't worry, Mother, she had finished under her breath, I won't be intruding on you and Daryl, not ever, but it won't be because of this Mr Malling.

The she had met Bruce.

Like most of her initial encounters, Clemmie mused now, even her encounter with Rickaby Roen, her first meeting with Bruce Malling had been through an animal. In this instance a dog.

She had been walking around the new project, approving the generous sections, so necessary for children, ponies and puppies, she had thought, when she had stopped to laugh at the gambolling of two spaniels. They must belong to the house round which they raced, the promotion partner's new home. She had hunched her shoulders.

Then she had noticed that the blue roan of the pair of spaniels was favouring one of his hind legs. It could be a fracture involving the thigh bone, had been Clemmie's first professional thought. She knew, from having regularly attended such injuries, how easily the accident occurred ... even a fall from a chair could cause it. She also knew that an owner, not knowledgeable about such things, would never dream that his dog was seriously hurt, and would put down any refusal to bear any weight on the limb to a mere pad scratch or a bruise, something that would mend itself in time.

Only it wouldn't mend, and Clemmie knew it. The dog would only ever step gently on the foot, possibly never step on it at all ad infinitum.

She had knelt down and called to the spaniel. He had come with that good humour that generally marks spaniels, and had submitted to Clemmie's examination.

The first Clemmie had been aware of Bruce Malling had been a shadow over the roan. Then he had spoken.

'I noticed Bingo carrying that foot and suspected a thorn or a stone bruise. He wouldn't let me near him to see, but you have the touch.'

'I try to.' Clemmie had glanced up, ready to dislike her parents' neighbour, and had met friendly russet eyes with her own blue, at first stormy, ones. She had seen fair curly hair, a boyish expression, a wide grin, a nice manner, and——

She had smiled back.

'Bruce Malling,' he had said.

'Clemmie.' Clemmie had left it at that. It had always been confusing, she had found, telling people she was a Green but her mother a Coyle.

'Is it a thorn, do you think? I've noticed there's a few bindi-eyes around. Could you get it out for Bingo and me?'

'I'm afraid it's more serious than that,' she told him, 'it's a fracture.'

'What?'

'A fracture. Fortunately' ... Clemmie's fingers had worked around the roan ... 'not a bad one.'

'Good lord, how would Bingo do such a thing?'

'You'd be surprised how easy it is. Even playing a little too robustly with the other fellow would do it.'

'You're a wonder,' he said admiringly. 'Can you recommend someone to me? I can't let him hop round like that.'

'Better still, I believe I can fix him. I'll need ...' Clemmie had recited her requirements.

It had all, she thought drearily now, gone on from there.

They had laughed a lot; you could almost say that laughter had been their basis. It had been Clemmie's basis, anyway. Suddenly she had realised how little, how very little she had laughed before in her life, and how sweet she had found this laughter.

Then something else had crept in, perhaps it had been only 'almost', as she was trying to convince herself now, but suddenly she had not felt lonely and empty any more, she had felt ... had felt ...

She gave a little start. A man's hand was feeling for her hand.

'Take it easy, kid,' Rickaby Roen said.

'I am—I mean, I'm trying. I mean, I will. Well—in time. I suppose you're thinking I'm a fool after I'd turned, or believed I turned, a page? closed a chapter?'

'Yes, you're a fool,' he agreed, 'but who wants a

wisehead? Like to come back to the house now and talk it out?'

'What is there to talk about?' she sighed.

'Everything, I'd say. To begin with, you have to make some gesture. You have to write, or ring ... or go.'

'Go?' She looked at him startled; was he sending her away after all they'd been through?

'Over there to your folks. Oh, no, I didn't mean go from here.' A soft little laugh.

'Why? Why must I?' But even as she said it Clemmie knew he was right. She had to contact the family, congratulate Amber ... wish Amber's fiancé the best.

'If you don't get in touch,' Rickaby was telling her, 'they'll think you're missing; even possibly contact the police.'

'Oh, no!' she protested.

'Clemmie, be serious,' he begged.

'I am serious. I've never even made a ripple at home. No, they wouldn't worry.'

'Eventually you would still cause quite a large and embarrassing wave. Anyway, they'd only take your silence as resentment, and I shouldn't think you'd want that.'

'No,' she agreed.

'Then write, ring or go.'

'What do you think?' Clemmie asked pitifully.

He said, 'Much against my will I advise you to go.'

'Against your will?'

'It's a risk. A risk for me.'

'What do you mean?' she queried.

'I told you before, that smoke in Malling's eyes. When he sees you again some of the Amber smoke might have cleared, and that I would not like.'

'Oh, you fool!' Clemmie snapped. After a moment she asked: 'Why should I go instead of write or ring?'

'Because it's more rounded. If you do the others it's not as full a gesture.'

'How wrong you are,' Clemmie said bitterly. 'They'll barely notice me.'

He looked at her a long perceptive moment; if Clemmie had looked back she would have been surprised at the understanding—and the gentleness—in his face.

'That bad?' he asked.

'Yes.'

'You poor child!' He put his arm around Clemmie. 'And I used to yearn for happy famblies, *any* famblies. Nonetheless, go, Clemmie. It will be more conclusive. I'm supposing, of course, that you want it like that. Concluded, I mean. If you don't, just say the word.'

'Why? Are you magic or something?'

'Or something,' he nodded. 'Yes, I could wipe the triumphant smile off your parents' face in a minute.'

'How?'

'By their favourite daughter ... yes, that's quite obvious of Amber ... *not* marrying as well as they're thinking with young Malling. Should I buy out Osborne at once?'

'Osborne will sell to Bruce.'

'Oh, no, not after my offer. Sentiment will dry up like dewdrops in the sun. And I'll do it immediately if you want it that way.'

'To spite my mother and stepfather?'

'To make you happy,' he replied. 'The little I knew of Amber assures me that she wouldn't want young Malling for love alone, so presto, unwanted, spurned, he returns to you.' He snapped his fingers and laughed.

'I thought you intended to confine Bruce to one-third regardless,' Clemmie said coldly.

'In time I intend to, but if you say the word now——'

'I don't say the word.'

He shrugged carelessly as though he was becoming uninterested.

'All right, then, the engagement stands. Are you writing, ringing or going?'

'You said to go,' she reminded him.

'Since when have you listened to me?'

'Now,' Clemmie told him. 'Amber is my sister and I would have to go, otherwise it might seem churlish.'

'Also inconclusive. Right, we've established that, but when? Are you too tired to leave at once?'

'No, not too tired, in fact anxious to get it over.'

'Then back to the house.' He walked a few steps, then stopped. 'You'll be home tonight?'

'It's not home, and no, I won't. I can't just put my head round a door and call out the best of everything, I'll have to stay a while.'

'A very little while,' Rickaby stipulated. 'You're in my employ now, remember, you can't go racing off here, there and everywhere like this.'

'It was your suggestion,' she reminded him.

'All the same ...' He began to walk again.

Clemmie caught up with him.

'Later on ... after I see my people ... I'll be living in my flat again and commuting out here,' she told him.

'It's a bit late, isn't it?'

'Late?'

'Convention,' he reminded her diabolically. 'The damage is done.'

'It isn't, and anyway you wouldn't ... you couldn't ...'

'I would. I could. But I won't. No, I'll let you return to your virtuous couch every evening. Well, for a time.'

'For all time,' said Clemmie firmly.

'We'll see.' They were at the old home now. 'I'm going down to inspect Clematis. You'll be gone when I come back.'

'Yes.'

'Drive carefully.'

'Yes.'

A pause. 'Don't care too much,' he said a little oddly.

This time Clemmie did not answer. She ran to her room.

Five minutes later she was backing Miss Muffett out of the old gates. Across the field Rickaby Roen raised an arm to her. Clemmie took a hand off the wheel and waved back to him. Then she started the ascent from the valley, the descent to the next valley, eventually the run to the coast, then the climb to another section of the hinterland, the Summer Heights Estate.

It was not until an hour later, not until she was nearing her parents' home, that nervousness caught up with her.

Why am I coming here? What shall I say? What will they say to me? How will I be able to meet Bruce?

She tried to steady herself by repeating that probably she would not see Bruce, anyway; just because an engagement notice was in the paper it did not mean he would be at the house.

But the moment she turned the Mini into the estate, she could see there was no hope of escaping that moment. The drive was jammed with cars; she would have to leave her own on the kerb. Or could she leave without being noticed, come at some less public time? About to turn, Clemmie saw it was too late. Someone was indicating a parking position to her, and to pay no attention would be to draw more attention to herself. She nodded a thanks to the person who had pointed out the vacancy in the row of cars, someone she had never seen before, and slid Miss Muffett into the space left between a Jaguar and a Bentley. Some visitors, she thought wryly, then ... as lights were switched on ... some party. For obviously it was a party. An engagement party? Yes, it would have to be that.

She waited until the desultory interest of the on-lookers curious about each new arrival found other sources, then slipped out of the Mini and ran into the house. She chose the back entrance as less obvious, and, sprinting across the lawn, turned the handle of the kitchen door.

The table inside was groaning with plates ready to be borne in, and standing regarding them was Alison.

'Mother,' Clemmie said.

Mrs Coyle turned, looked surprised and displeased for the briefest of moments, then evidently decided to treat her elder daughter as a blessing, not a bane.

'Clementine! Thank heaven for you.'

'Yes, Mother?'

'Those wretched caterers,' sighed her mother, 'they've certainly prepared a fine spread, but so far no one has turned up to do the serving.'

'They will, and if they don't, I'm here. I take it' ... a pause ... 'that it's an engagement party.'

'A betrothal tea.' That would be Daryl, full of

Victorian elegance. 'Yes, dear. We would have let you know, of course, but we didn't know where to find you. How did you learn of it? But through the newspaper announcement, I suppose.'

'Yes, through the announcement. I was going to ring, then I thought' ... no, actually Rickaby had thought, Clemmie recalled ... 'it would be nicer to see my sister personally, give her my good wishes personally.'

'Of course, dear, though the other would still have done as well, indeed I believe Daryl——' A slight frown. 'But I'm sure Daryl will be as pleased as I am to have you by us, Clementine, in the event that the waitresses don't arrive. Oh, yes, you're very welcome, dear. You never said where you were working. You must tell us tomorrow. Tonight, of course, is dear Amber's night. You do' ... a little uncertainly ... 'understand that?'

'I understand perfectly, Mother. The best man has won. And now do you mind if I slip along and congratulate the best man—meaning the best girl, of course. My sister Amber.'

'Do that, dear. Then come back here, unless, that is, you see that the hired staff have arrived.'

'I promise.' Clemmie slipped out of the room and down the passage.

The corridor to the dormitory quarters took Clemmie out of view of the guests but past her stepfather's office. The lights were on in his room, she saw, but she took little notice; tonight was a special occasion, so all the lights would be on. It was Amber's ... and Bruce's ... engagement party. No, betrothal tea, Clemmie corrected dully; Mr Coyle preferred betrothal. About to slip past the door, voices inside the room halted her. It would be hard slipping past, she realised, and she stood silent a moment wondering what she should do. In spite of her mother's reassurance that her stepfather would not be unpleased to see her, Clemmie felt that until he learned about the kitchen predicament he certainly would not be pleased. She hesitated, and into the hesitation drifted three voices, one a man's voice she did not know, one a woman's voice she did not know, and her stepfather's.

'I'm sure' ... it was Daryl, mellifluously ... 'I've never known a happier moment; this moment of my darling daughter's betrothal to your son, my dear Mr and Mrs Malling, has reached the heights.'

'Jean ... George,' the Mallings were murmuring. Clemmie heard the chink of glasses.

George Malling said: 'But daughter, Daryl? I was told ... I trust I don't offend ... that Amber was——'

'My stepdaughter? True. And no offence. But I love her like a daughter.' Another chink.

'There is another stepdaughter, I believe.' It was the woman's voice.

'Yes, Jean. Clementine.' Daryl left it at that.

'Well' ... still the woman ... 'if she's anything like Amber ... What a beauty!'

'Clementine is not.'

'Still,' came in George Malling shrewdly, 'beauty is as beauty does, isn't that so, Daryl? In other words, has Amber—will she—I mean——'

'Has she anything to bring besides her beauty?'

'Now I didn't say that,' reproved George Malling.

'But I know what's on your mind, and believe me it would be the same with me, but let me assure you now that Amber will come most satisfactorily placed.'

'I know you've done well,' George Malling broke in, 'Bruce told us that.'

'I have. And later on it will all be Amber's.'

'. . . But what about the other girl?'

'Well, Clemintine is an entirely different person, not at all like Amber. She follows her own path. She would be totally uninterested in anything like this. Hence' . . . a deprecating cough . . . 'her non-appearance now.'

'But surely that's not a reason for cutting her out of a will, if I'm taking you the right way.'

'You are, but Clementine is one of your modern rebels, a rebel, for instance, against money.'

'Oh, we know that sort. Then Amber will——'

'Exactly. Also, as well as what Alison and I could bequeath her there will be some money from her aunt.'

'Left to Amber?'

'To my dear wife. But as I said, Jean and George——'

'Of course.' More clinks. 'You don't mind us probing like this, do you? We've done it for all of our boys.'

'I approve of it. I would do likewise. Can I top you up?' Clemmie heard the decanter at work again.

'And what,' asked Daryl Coyle in his turn, 'is Bruce's position?'

'Admirable. It was a bit of a setback having Fitzroy sell out his third, it means now that Bruce must assure himself of Osborne's third to gain a monopoly, but I have no doubt it can be done.'

'No doubt at all, he's a very astute boy. We, my wife and I, are very pleased with him.'

'Let's drink to that,' Clemmie heard, and she took the opportunity to dash past the door and run down the corridor to the bedrooms. If she knew her sister, Amber had not made her appearance yet. Amber would wait until the final guest arrived, and then walk in.

Clemmie tapped on the door, heard Amber's 'Come in' and did so.

Amber sat at her dressing table doing lovely subtle things to her lips and eyes.

'Hi,' she said.

Clemmie crossed over and kissed her sister, careful not to muss her. To her surprise Amber did not peer petulantly into the mirror for any disarray, something she always did, and she actually caught, if briefly, at Clemmie's hand.

'Oh, Clemmie!' she exclaimed.

'Congratulations,' said Clemmie.

'You're not ... well ...'

'No, dear.'

'I'm glad.' A pause. 'He's nice.'

'Very,' Clemmie agreed.

'Do you know what, Clemmie, I think I've even' ... a pause ... 'fallen for him. Me!' A little incredulous laugh.

'Then don't hurt him, Amber,' Clemmie said quickly, and apologised at once.

But Amber was a different Amber tonight. Instead of flashing back an angry rejoinder, as she always did, she said quietly: 'No, I wouldn't want to hurt Bruce, not ever. But' ... one of those Amber-smiles that did things to people ... 'I wouldn't want to hurt you, either. Not that I wouldn't, Clemmie. Not when it comes to Bruce. I—well, I feel like I've never felt before.'

'Then, darling, you have my blessing,' smiled Clemmie.

'That's corny, but I like it.' Again Amber said incredulously: 'Me!'

Before Clemmie could answer, Amber asked, not waiting for a reply as she always did: 'How is your new place of work? Where is it? Any likely prospects? Are you staying overnight? Do you think everyone would have arrived by now?'

'There were crowds of cars when I arrived.' Clemmie only answered the last.

'A lot of the Mallings' friends flew up from Melbourne. You can imagine what the wedding will be.' A little laugh.

'And when will it be?' Clemmie asked, hoping she was keeping her voice steady.

'Soon. Clemmie, do you mind buzzing out now? I think it's time I made my big entrance, and you do look a bit—well——'

'I came straight from the stud,' Clemmie explained. 'We had trouble with a sick filly, at least she wasn't sick, she met with an accident, and——'

'I'm sure.' Amber did not disguise her boredom. This was the Amber that Clemmie knew, so she did not take offence.

'I'll join the admiring crowd,' she said.

'Do. How do I look?'

'As you always look.'

'Tonight it has to be even better,' said Amber, and she peered at herself in the mirror, a vision in gold. What had Rickaby said? Gold for Amber. He had described her as leaf green, Clemmie thought. If he could see her dishevelment now he would change that to dun. She slipped out, careful to stand behind the crowds, and in the concealment of one of the large potted palms that must have been brought in for the occasion.

Waiters now were moving around with trays of drinks, and waitresses with plates of savouries. So the caterers had arrived. Clemmie was glad of that, both for Alison and for herself, for now she need not mingle. She could just stand here, wait for an opportunity to congratulate Bruce, greet her stepfather, then go.

Clemmie stepped further back behind the tall palm, avoiding a waiter's eye, a waitress's attention, letting the talk drift round her.

A small orchestra began to play, ostensibly a background to the babble of conversation, but really, Clemmie knew, to be there to change their light strains into something more arresting the moment Amber walked in. The crowd knew it, too, or at least the Coyle guests knew their Daryl and how he did things, for the talk was only intermittent now, everyone seemed waiting. Bruce, too, was waiting. Between the palm banners Clemmie watched him, and she knew an ache of love surging through her, and after it an emptiness that left her so depleted she had to grab at one of the branches for support. The movement set the leaves stirring, and, arrested by the motion in a closed room, Bruce looked across the sea of people and saw Clemmie. For a moment their eyes met, Bruce's russet, Clemmie's blue. The man made an instinctive step forward and his hand half-rose.

Then the rhythm of the music was changing to an entry theme, the raising, as it were, of a curtain, and the golden girl was coming in. Amber. Gold for Amber.

At once, with all the other eyes, Bruce was looking at the glorious being that had come among them. There was a triumph of possession in his face, a kind of 'Can this be happening to me?' ... almost a disbelief at so much beauty, so much charm. For him.

Clemmie saw her stepfather moving forward, heard his honeyed voice break smoothly into the music which at once ceased, heard the words that she knew, being Daryl Coyle, Daryl would have rehearsed a dozen times.

'Dear ladies and gentlemen, dear friends, for friends of George and Jean Malling must be my friends, too, it is now my very precious task to announce ...'

Clemmie slipped out.

She found it surprisingly easy to escape from the house. Only the waiters and waitresses were in the hall, and they were too busy to wonder at a guest who evidently had heard all this before. They passed her with their trays, not even glancing at her. Clemmie left the house by the back entrance, ran nimbly across to her Mini and set off at once.

It was not until she was descending to the coast that she remembered she had not congratulated Bruce, had not presented herself to Daryl Coyle. But ... negotiating a sharp mountain bend ... neither would even notice. Indeed, her stepfather would not have been pleased to see her; perhaps if there had been a mix-up in the catering he would not have minded a helping hand, but apart from that he would have preferred her absence. What had he said to the Mallings? 'Clementine is an entirely different person. She follows her own path. She would be totally uninterested in anything like this. Hence her non-appearance now.' Oh, no, an appearance after all would not be to Daryl's liking.

Then Bruce, too, would take no notice. Clemmie shut her eyes a moment at the memory of that incredulous look on Bruce's face, that—that dazzlement. Oh, Bruce ... wisely Clemmie had opened her eyes again ... how could you not be dazzled—after me?

She became aware, from the wavering street lamps, that tears were watering all the lights, that she was crying. A little angrily she wiped her sleeve across her eyes, but the tears kept coming, kept restricting her view.

She ran through Surfers Paradise, intending to keep travelling up the coast to her Brisbane apartment, stop there the night. But presently she found that instinctively she had taken the Sperry Stud turn-off and was travelling west instead. Indeed, she had come almost all the way.

This would not do. She could not return tonight, give Rickaby Roen an account of it all, for an account that man certainly would demand.

Still slightly blinded, Clemmie began to do a U-turn, foolish, she knew, when one did not know the road, but she was in too much of a hurry to get out and examine the road first.

She was not lucky. At once she went into a ditch. At daylight she knew she could have manoeuvred the small car out again, but in the dark of night, not helped by her wet eyes, she descended with a bump, and stopped there.

'Oh, no!' she cried vexedly. She cut the engine and climbed out of the car. She found she was imprisoned as neatly as if the ditch had been built around her, no hope of doing anything tonight.

She leaned against the Mini, wondering what she could do.

Walk the rest of the way to Sperry was the obvious
answer, but it was not what she had attempted that
disastrous U-turn for. She had wanted to get away
from questions, away from estimating eyes. Oh, damn,
her own eyes were letting her down again, once more
they were streaming tears. Bruce, Bruce, you were the
first and now you'll be the last. Bruce, why did you ...
why didn't you ... why ... why ...

'Are you all right?' The voice cut sharply into
Clemmie's self-pity. She peered into the darkness ...
she had switched off the lights ... and in the faint star-
light she recognised Rickaby Roen.

'How did you——' she began.

'Know it was you? I didn't. I was standing at the
window and I saw the car beam stop suddenly, and
guessed something was wrong. So I came across. How
in heaven did you get in this position?'

'I was coming back,' she explained.

'Before you came?'

'I hadn't intended to come.'

'No, I had expected you'd be staying overnight at
your home.'

'My stepfather's home,' she corrected.

He hunched his shoulders. 'But you didn't,' he said.

'No. I decided to go to my flat.'

'Out here?' Now his brows had risen.

'I don't know how I came to be out here, I—I just
seem to have come spontaneously.'

'That's understandable,' he said dryly.

'You mean the filly?'

He did not answer that.

'I turned back,' said Clemmie wretchedly, 'and I'm
afraid I made rather a mess of it.'

'That would be the understatement of the year,'

There was a small laugh. 'A team of men and a crane will be needed to get it out. But so long as you're not hurt—— You aren't hurt, Clemmie?' He made a step forward.

'No, I'm not hurt,' Clemmie said quickly.

'Is that a protesting note I hear? Protesting against me coming a step nearer? Methinks the lady doth protest too much. Perhaps she *is* hurt. Perhaps I'd better see for myself.' Now he made more than a step forward, he came right up to her, close to her, breath-close, heart-close. She could even hear his heart.

All at once the utter maleness of him was too much to bear. As naturally as if he was her lover, Clemmie reached up to him and put her arms around him, touched his lips with hers.

'Rickaby,' she said.

There was a silence, quite a lengthy one. Rickaby Roen broke it.

'In romantic books it would be "Bruce" and in your emotion you would be mistaking me for him, then regretting it later.' He said it laconically, detachedly, almost without interest.

'Rickaby.' Clemmie spoke instinctively again, not knowing why she did, but still saying it.

Then she felt his arms tighten around her, imprison her, hold her.

'I could love you to oblivion for that,' Rickaby was whispering in her ear, 'if I weren't too old and too wise and too knowing. Just what happened at Summer Heights tonight?'

'Nothing. Oh, there was an announcement, but—nothing.'

'You ask me to believe that?' He was still closer than close, so close that she could hear the barely perceptible but still harsh undertone in his voice as he questioned her. As she did not answer he insisted: 'Tell me, Clemmie.'

'Nothing. Only——'

'Only?' he persisted.

'Only I saw him across the room.'

'Malling?'

'Yes.'

'And?'

'Nothing,' she said again. 'Oh, Rickaby ... Rickaby ...' She pressed close to him once more.

For several minutes he let her stay there, then deliberately he unfastened her hands, one finger at a time, until he was released.

'I'm a fool,' he said thickly, 'any man must be a fool who passes up such a chance. But my name is Roen, Clemmie, not Malling.'

'I know that,' she said quietly.

'Your tongue knows it, but not your heart. You're only talking with your tongue, never your heart.'

'But——' she began.

'One day you're going to be my wife, I told you that. But it will only be when a ghost has been laid, when not even a shadow or an echo or a memory remains. Do you think I'd ever share my bed with two people?'

'I never said——' she began.

'You did, though. You offered yourself just now, offered yourself—along with your sister's husband.'

'He isn't that,' she said. 'Not yet.'

'I note that you're not arguing about your offer,' he observed.

'I didn't ... I mean ... oh, Rickaby, I'm so unhappy I feel I could fill eternity with my sorrow.'

'Then fill it, don't take it out on me. Not that I don't

want what you have, but I'm older now, and I can wait. It will make it all the sweeter when it does happen, Clemmie.

'Now, back to the house with you and into bed. *Your* bed.'

'I——' she began.

'No, no cajoling, no enticing. I don't want you.'

'If you think I meant that——'

'I know you meant that, not knowingly perhaps, but the instinct was still there, the need to be wanted, soothed. But I've never been, and I don't intend to begin now, a woman's comforter. Also I don't plan to play second fiddle. When it comes to my woman I have to be first, last and in between, I have to be the sole one, the entirety. I think it's best that you realise that at once. On which note' ... as Clemmie tried to break in ... 'we will conclude this scene. We will go back, and when you wake up in the morning it will be to find another couple in the house. I've signed on a handyman and his wife. With such an amorous strapper around' ... an ironic bow ... 'I had to protect myself. No, none of that.' He caught at Clemmie's upstretched palm and held it. 'Unless,' he warned, 'you want it back much harder than you gave. You're distraught, you're upset, you're not functioning properly, and you're going to feel sorry about a whole heap of things in the morning. But attacking me won't help any more than seducing me to spite Bruce would have helped. Try some other time when I'm not in such a virtuous mood. I might take you up on it then. No, cancel that— I *will* take you up on it. That's a promise, not a threat.

'I put some milk on to heat before I came over,' he went on. 'I rather suspected those car lights would be yours. When we get back you'll have some and go straight to bed to sleep.'

'Sleep?' disbelieved Clemmie.

'All the same I think you will.' He was hustling her over the grass, helping her over rough patches, lifting her over the gate. As they approached the house, he took her right up in his arms and carried her.

He placed her in her bed, left her but was back almost at once with the promised milk.

'Not undressed yet? Do you want me to help?'

'No, I don't!' she said crossly.

'Funny, and yet ten minutes ago——'

'I didn't! You're exaggerating things. You——'

'Drink your milk,' he ordered. 'Undress or stay dressed, please yourself, but get to bed.' Without another word he left.

Muttering angrily, Clemmie drank the milk. It tasted different—probably laced with something. But it was not laced with whisky or brandy, she knew that at once, neither would have made her instantly drowsy like this.

For she removed nothing, not even her shoes. She just lay down, and that was it.

When she opened her eyes again it was morning, and not, looking at her watch, early morning. Rickaby must have put a sedative in that drink, enough to knock her out. A pity it had not knocked out her memories now. Clemmie lay remembering what had taken place between them, what she had said. What he had refused. 'Oh, no!' she said aloud in horror.

'But I think you should.' The speaker was a pleasant-looking, middle-aged woman, and she must have come in while Clemmie was absorbed in her humiliating thoughts.

A steaming cup of coffee was being put into Clemmie's hand, and the woman was saying something about a hot bath waiting, and after that breakfast, and that her name was Rachel, her husband Gavin.

Clemmie took a scalding sip from the cup and said Yes, Yes, Yes.—Something, she thought wretchedly, *he* had not said. Rickaby Roen had politely rejected her, and she was very thankful to him.—Well, she was, wasn't she?

Anyway, she was thankful to Rachel, and said so. She drank the coffee, undressed ... mad to undress after a night's sleep instead of vice versa ... put on her dressing gown and went along to the bath. As she lay back in the water she wondered how she would face Roen this morning.

She need not have worried. When eventually she went to the kitchen, only one place was set—hers.

'Mr Roen has gone. He won't be back for several weeks. Something needing his attention in the west, he said. But he left a note.' Rachel handed it to Clemmie.

Clemmie deliberately did not open it until she had finished eating. Then she tore open the envelope and scanned the first letter she had received from Rickaby Roen.

'Dear Wife,' it began.

CHAPTER SIX

THE nerve of him! The colossal nerve of that arrogant, browbeating roughrider of a man! Clemmie sat fuming for a second, then, unwillingly but inevitably, she grinned. The grin grew into a giggle, the giggle into helpless laughter. Rachel, evidently hearing the mirth, put her head round the door and smiled at Clemmie.

'He is a funny person,' she agreed, taking it for granted that Clemmie was chuckling over something in the letter. 'He was telling Gavin and me all about bringing you in from the old gold shaft' ... not *all*, Clemmie hoped ... 'and we had to smile. It must have been awful for you, dear, but then with a man like Mr Roen——'

'Yes. A man like Mr Roen.' Clemmie waited for Rachel to withdraw, then she returned to the letter.

'Dear Wife, By the time you will be reading this I shall be flying west. Much as I love my new promotion, and who comes with it' ... who, indeed! ... 'business is still business, especially if I'm to build up Sperry as you advise, and particularly so if I wish to top any offer Malling makes for Osborne's third in Summer Heights.

'I can't say how long I'll be away, so don't do anythink you wouldn't care to be surprised at. (Like last night?)' Clemmie squirmed.

'You will now have met the good Rachel, and soon, no doubt, the good Gavin. Rachel will take over the house for you, and Gavin, who comes with excellent

121

references if no diplomas, will be a tower of strength on the stock side. I've left him with an open cheque to start building up our numbers, and with his expertise and your touch I'm expecting wonderful things, even a Melbourne Cupper. I'm not serious over that last, of course, but I'll be looking for some improvements round the place.

'That's all for now, Clemmie. Forgive the presumptuous opening ... not really presumptuous, as you and I know. You see, I, too, get carried away at times.' I, too. Again Clemmie squirmed.

'Thine, R.'

Thine! Clemmie put the note down. This time she did not laugh, but she did not fume either. She looked at the letter a long odd moment, then pocketed it and went out to Rachel.

It would be a relief, she knew, to have the domestic side taken off her hands. Even though she had told Rickaby that first daughters can invariably cook, Clemmie had no reluctance to passing over the chore to Rachel. If breakfast, and the luncheon dish she was now preparing, were anything to go by, Sperry was going to be well fed. She asked Rachel where to find her husband, and, being told the west paddock, made her way there.

Gavin Tomelly was leaning over a rail regarding Sperry's stock, for by this time the filly had joined the others. He smiled as Clemmie joined him, and touched a wide hat.

'Well?' asked Clemmie.

'Is that a question?' Gavin asked ruefully. 'If so the answer is not well. Oh, not the girls and boys themselves, they're quite all right, but the meagre number. Rick needs much more.'

'He must realise that,' Clemmie said, 'because he's told me he's left you a blank cheque, meaning he wants you to do some shopping.'

'You, too. Rick was adamant on that. Equal to a vet, he told me.' Gavin crinkled friendly grey eyes on Clemmie.

'I don't believe he told you quite that,' she smiled.

'No, the same as he couldn't tell you I was a degree man, but he'd know all the same that I was well aware what should go with four legs.'

'So he left you an open cheque to find something.'

'Left *us* an open cheque. You're to shop with me. Now, what I thought was this——'

By the time Rachel called out lunch, Gavin and Clemmie had agreed on their purchases, where they would purchase them, how far they would commit Roen.

'Lunch!' called Rachel again across the paddock. 'How many times do you have to be told?'

'Not once more,' laughed Clemmie to Gavin, 'even this far away that aroma has defeated me.' She ran to the old homestead and washed. As the cool water splashed over her wrists she thought incredulously, could this be the same miserable girl who had walked out of an engagement party, walked out only last night? ... Deliberately Clemmie did not think of what had come after that ...

She hurried to the old eat-in kitchen and the large pie Rachel had put on the table.

Gavin came in and sat down, and the talk went, as it always did, Clemmie recalled from the stud attendances she had made with Lindsay, to horses, then horses, then after that horses.

Gavin was no vet, and being less-than-grad herself

Clemmie appreciated the practical good sense he brought to the work he had chosen. Rachel, probably as generally knowledgeable on the subject as her husband, put in her findings, and the talk flashed between the three, opinions on pedal bones, how vegetable extract, dextrose and calcium could, if necessary, take the place of a mother, how Rickaby should lay down some sand rolls. Most of all ... forks aloft in excitement ... the yearling sales coming up at which Gavin intended to spend all or some of Roen's open cheque.

'Yes, it's on tomorrow, Clem,' Gavin said, 'and we'll be there for the first bid. It's not far away, in fact we'll be able to tow back any purchases, this Sperry, I have found, being sadly short of a float.'

'No float?' said Clemmie in disapproval.

'Only one that Noah must have used. Definitely unsafe, and' ... with disgust ... 'no view for the traveller.'

Clemmie agreed heartily with that. She felt strongly about stall windows at the right level, and floats with look-outs so that a horse could enjoy the countryside.

During the afternoon chores Gavin sought out Clemmie. He wore a wide grin.

'Seems like some of our re-population worries are over,' he told her.

'You've bought something already?'

'No, but our brown girl is pregnant. Not looking for it before, I hadn't noticed it. I expect it was the same with you.'

'Yes,' laughed Clemmie in surprise, 'but now you draw my attention ... when would you say, Gavin?'

'Having left things to nature, in other words no records written down in a book, it's hard to tell precisely. But I should think it mightn't be all that far off.'

'I wonder who sired it,' she mused.

'You have only two guesses,' shrugged Gavin, 'unless a brumby called in. But there'll be more material in the future if we find anything promising at the sale.'

'What are you after?' Clemmie asked.

'What I can get, but two girls and two boys would be handy. The stud putting on the auction is an old and dependable one, and best of all only some twenty kilometres if you take a back track I happen to know. Name of Fethering. You may have heard of it.'

Clemmie nodded that she had.

Rachel would not come to the sale the next morning; she said she had had enough of four-footed sales, but if Gavin would suggest a two-footed one . . .

'If we make a good buy at Fethering I'll take you in to the Brisbane sales,' Gavin promised. 'Clemmie will hold the fort here for the day. Ready, Clem?'

'Yes.' There was no preparation needed for a country yearling sale, Clemmie knew, and, apart from her jodhpurs and shirt, she simply wore her own freshly scrubbed face, bright eyes and wind-swept hair.

Everything was bright emerald down in the valleys, as befitted stud country, approved Clemmie, enjoying the scenery if not her rather bumpy seat beside Gavin, but the hills they climbed were cigar-leaf and gold from the rain run-off, except the higher mountains that leaned bruise blue against a heraldic sky.

As they approached Fethering, Clemmie felt a thrill she had known several times by the side of Lindsay, the sight of cars and lorries and floats drawn up on a quiet country road that generally knew little or even no traffic, the unaccustomed sight of people, the sound of bid and of hammer.

'First we take a look,' said Gavin.

'For what?'

'I think you know as well as I do,' he grinned, and Clemmie did. Lindsay had drilled into her the desirable qualities to look for, and she looked for them now ... found to her gratification that her choice coincided with Gavin's.

'We'll bid for Jiminy Cricket, Lulu's Girl, Big Boy and John L., then,' Gavin declared.

'Can the open cheque be stretched that far?'

'I reckon bidding for four should at least give us two,' said Gavin hopefully.

He ... they ... were lucky. They secured three, at very reasonable prices. At first Clemmie felt they would be going home empty-handed, for the bidding started high, but it found its own level, and they managed all of their choices except John L. who proved too pricey.

'A future Melbourne Cupper, that bloke,' said Gavin, accepting his other purchases and attaching them to long reins from the back of the car. 'It's a crude way of delivering them home, but I reckon, seeing it's only a short distance, we should manage the tow safely enough. What do you think, Clem?'

'Yes, but take it very easy,' Clemmie advised.

It was probably because of the ease with which they brought the three back to Sperry that they finally finished up with four newcomers instead, one a strictly illegitimate guest. It was a very young vixen, and Gavin found it in the mouth of its unfortunate mother, who, evidently unused to the traffic that the sale had inspired, had been run over as she crossed the narrow road, and had died with her baby still securely held.

'I'll keep it in a warm room and bottle-feed it,' said Clemmie, cuddling the bewildered little thing.

'And the law will want to know all about it,' agreed Gavin laconically.

'They needn't know,' she pointed out.

'But what will you do when it grows out of warm rooms and bottles? What will you do with it when Rick finds out?'

'Point taken, but I'll still mind her for a while.' They were turning into Sperry gates now, and their purchases looked none the worse for their tow.

'Let's hope they settle in just as well,' said Gavin, 'I'm expecting the beginnings of a dynasty here.'

'Any special mating?'

'I'll leave it to you to match the good points and minimise the bad. Just so long,' Gavin smiled, 'as we begin to expand.'

'Don't forget our brown girl is doing that right now —expanding.'

'Yes. I'll have a look at her after I take this lot down. You go in, Clem.'

'Can't I help?' she asked.

'Not with that young 'un in your arms.'

Clemmie laughed, and carried the orphan into Sperry. Rachel, being a country person, if not exactly approving was also not aghast.

'I suppose it's all right while she's little,' she shrugged.

When Gavin came up from the paddock he reported everyone happy, but added a little warily that he and Clemmie might soon not be.

'Why?' Clemmie demanded.

'That brown girl is much closer than I estimated,' he told her. 'She has one of those builds that fools you into believing it's further off than you think.'

'And on second examination it's not?'

'Not,' Gavin agreed. 'How are you on lantern and torch deliveries?'

'Seriously?'

'Seriously. Still, we have the rest of the day yet.'

But Brown Girl ... they were calling her that now ... did not oblige them by a daylight delivery, so they began to hope instead she would hold off until tomorrow. That did not happen, either. At midnight, Gavin tapped on Clemmie's door, Rachel behind him with lanterns and flasks and rugs, and Clemmie knew it was on. She checked on the baby vixen, then followed Gavin's torchlight across to the corner of the paddock where Brown Girl was awaiting her blessed event.

Right from the beginning everything went wrong. Brown Girl had a high body temperature and it was apparent it would not be an easy birth. So long, Gavin sighed once, as it was not an endless one. He doubted if the mare would stand that.

Fortunately it was not long, but it was an unhappy event, for the foal, at first glance put on the danger list, succumbed in a short time.

It was a sad beginning for a recovering stud, and Clemmie knew Gavin was feeling as wretched as she was. More, she supposed, for being a man he did not have that luxury of tears that she and Rachel had over the little dead foal.

It was a disenchanted trio who came back to the homestead in the early hours of the morning to try to slip in a little sleep before the demands of another day.

Demands there were. The Brown Girl did not recover as she should, even taking into consideration her difficult confinement, and Gavin and Clemmie decided that if the mare was to survive ... and suddenly

it became the most important thing in the world that
one of the two still breathed ... that she would have
to be held up. If she got down, she would stay down,
they agreed, she would surely follow her dead foal.

They took turns in doing this, in holding her erect,
Rachel assisting Clemmie, Gavin holding her unaided,
right through to the following morning. The only
thing that got them through was the knowledge, just
by looking at Brown Girl, that her chances of survival
were improving every minute.

Improving rapidly, too, was the young vixen;
Clemmie felt sure it had grown an inch in a day. At
this rate she would have to do some serious thinking
about her. She could not put the little thing back in
the bush without the guidance of a mother, but where
else could the baby go?

Gavin came to the rescue with the suggestion that
he leave it at the animal farm on the coast; the vixen
would be safe there, even pampered, her only require-
ment not to mind the admiration of the paying public
who visited the farm.

'Yes, but when?' asked Clemmie dubiously, convinced that the vixen had just added another inch.

'That's the crunch,' Gavin laughed. 'Do you remember promising me you'd hold the fort while I
took Rachel to the two-footed sales?'

'Actually you said it, Gavin, but of course I will. So
it's to be goodbye, darling.' Clemmie patted the vixen's
head.

The three left the next morning, and Clemmie
found time racing by as she performed the hundred
and one tasks of a stud. But the hard work exhilarated
her, for the first time in a long time she found herself
thinking of today and tomorrow instead of looking

back at yesterday. She did not even pause, scarlet-faced, to remember her episode on the night of the engagement. She simply fed, watered, checked, watched, went through it all again.

But Brown Girl worried her every time she looked at her. Though she had recovered, Clemmie never had seen such a depressed, desolate creature. Thinking it might brighten her up, Clemmie had returned her to the general paddock to be with the others, but nothing, it seemed, could brighten Brown Girl. Sad-faced, she withdrew from the grass-picking, contented group to slink miserably round the rim of the fence, occasionally giving a feed bin a kick to show how she felt. If she hadn't been desperately sorry for her, Clemmie would have returned Brown Girl to her convalescent quarters again with a reprimanding word.

Instead she fondled the lank-looking hair and patted the dejected head. 'Next time,' she tried to cheer. Still discouraged, the mare watched Clemmie return to the house.

There was nothing to do until watering time in the evening, so Clemmie kicked off her yard shoes, took the radio out to the verandah and found a soft chair.

The distance at this time of day was blue and swimmy, the radio music sweet, and Clemmie was only a breath away from sleep when the message alerted her. It was the Country Hour, and the appeal came from a distraught studmaster not far from Sperry. He had just gained a little colt but unhappily lost its mother. Could anyone help?

Clemmie was out of the chair in a shot. She knew Everley; it was only half an hour away if you took an old track. She felt confident she could be there before any other applicant. She felt confident, too, that Brown

Girl could make it comfortably, in fact the exercise should do her good.

It did not do Clemmie much good, though. Driving *and* towing, even at a dead slow pace, proved much harder than she had thought. But she made it, and she and Brown Girl were warmly greeted by Everley, who were about to make up a compound of powdered milk and water.

'But I'd sooner,' the studmaster said firmly, 'have the real stuff.'

Brown Girl wanted to give it, too ... Clemmie wanted her to. But, the way it sometimes is, and Clemmie could have shaken the snooty little colt, the small thing did not take to Brown Girl, to her lank hair, to her obvious lack of class, and he stuck up his nose and walked away.

They tried again and again, but eventually it became obvious even to Clemmie that here was no solution for her mare. Not far from tears, she refused a cup of tea and began the tow home again, even slower this time, for the mare had already done it once, and also Brown Girl *knew*. Knew she was rejected, thus dejected. Poor mother-of-nothing, Clemmie grieved.

When she reached Sperry she took Brown Girl back to the paddock. Only time now, she knew, would heal. She did not try 'Next time' again on the mare for the simple reason that she could not see her. Tears were not only blurring Clemmie's eyes, they were coursing down her cheeks.

That was how she ran into Rickaby. Concerned with her worries, she did not hear him approach, blinded by grief she did not see him. She ran directly into him, and the impact was like hitting a hard column of rock. She heard him curse, felt him even begin to shake her in his infuriation, then he must have seen her unhappy little face with its tumbling tears, for he stopped and kissed her instead.

It was a kiss like no other kiss that Clemmie ever had received, she had never dreamed there could be such concern, such gentleness. As his lips kissed each eyelid, kissed each ear, the hollow of her neck, and then her lips, Clemmie thought longingly that children would be kissed like this by their parents. Only she had not been.

She could not remember her mother ever kissing her like that, always her kisses had been hurried, perfunctory, something to be got over. Perhaps her father had kissed her like that, she could not remember. She did not realise she was speaking her thoughts aloud until Rickaby said quietly: 'I'm sure he did, I'm sure he kissed you like that all the time.'

'I don't know.'

'Then know this.' He kissed her gently again.

Presently he disengaged her and said, 'That's only for occasions like this, though, my other kisses will be very different, Clemmie, and please don't take that as a threat. Tell me' . . . turning her back to the homestead . . . 'what are the tears for? Have Rachel and Gavin deserted you? Where are they?'

'At a two-footed sale,' Clemmie said foolishly. 'No, I was crying for Brown Girl. You see, her foal died.'

'Foal?' he said in surprise. 'I didn't know——'

'Neither did we until it was imminent. Sometimes it's like that. Gavin suspected it first . . . that was before we went across to the yearling sale and bought the new stock.'

'Did you now?' he commented.

'Didn't you see?'

'I saw only a waterfall,' he grinned. 'But go on.'

'When we came back with them ... Jiminy Cricket, Lulu's Girl and Big Boy ... Brown Girl started having her pains.' A new flood of tears threatened. 'Everything went wrong.'

'Would you sooner leave it till later?' Rickaby was reaching for a handkerchief.

'No, now. It was a difficult birth, and the little one died almost at once.'

'It happens, Clemmie, and at least you saved the mother.'

'For what?' burst out Clemmie. 'Look back, Rickaby, did you ever see such a wretched bit of horse-flesh? She's utterly miserably, utterly—utterly rejected.'

'You mean dejected.'

'No, rejected. You see, the orphan foal wouldn't accept her. I heard this urgent message over the radio for a wet nurse and I took Brown Girl over.'

'I think you mean you and Gavin took her over,' he corrected.

'No, they'd gone to Brisbane ... oh, everything was all right then, no need to stop here. Well, I took her.'

'How?'

'I towed her. Very gently, I assure you.'

'Driving at the same time?'

'Yes.'

'And when you got there?'

'That snooty little colt wouldn't have anything to do with her. She turned away, and nothing would bring her back. Oh, Rickaby, I'm so miserable for her!'

They had reached the homestead now, and Rickaby was pulling Clemmie in, closing the door behind them.

'I think,' he said shrewdly, 'some of your misery is for yourself.'

'I suppose so,' she sighed. 'I'm rejected, too, in a way, aren't I?'

He did not answer, and something in his silence reached Clemmie. *Touched* her. 'Aren't I?' she asked again, waiting for the kindly denials he always gave her, his assurances that as soon as the smoke got out of Bruce's eyes he would be coming to Clemmie again. But Clemmie waited in vain. Presently Rickaby said:

'Rejected? Yes.'

'I am rejected.' She gave him another chance to deny it.

'Yes,' he agreed.

'You—you never said so before,' she said flatly.

'Look here, Clemmie,' he demanded, 'how long do you expect me to stand and tell lies to you?'

'Lies?'

'That's what I said.'

'Were they lies before?' she asked.

'Put it that, I didn't know before.'

'Know what, Rickaby?'

'That I hadn't read a paper.'

'What paper?'

'Tonight's.' He nodded to the table. 'They didn't waste much time, did they?' he asked. 'I always thought there was a lapse between an engagement and a marriage.'

'A marriage?' she gasped.

'Marriage is what I said.'

'Then it's happened?'

'It's happening within a few weeks.'

'It's in the paper?'

'Yes.'

'Yet they haven't told me,' she said bitterly.

'They probably still don't know your address.'

A few moments went by. 'They couldn't, could they?' Clemmie asked piteously.

'Know your address?'

'Marry. Marry—unless I knew.'

'Oh, don't be silly!' he snapped.

'But they couldn't,' she persisted.

'They have . . . at least they will.' Rickaby crossed to the table and took up the paper.

He did not open it at once. He said casually: 'I'm back before I planned. Have you noticed?'

'I want to hear what's written, Rickaby,' Clemmie insisted.

'Can't you read . . . no, I see you can't.' For the tears had started again.

'Tell me, please.'

'No. Oh, all right, then.' A turning of sheets.

'The marriage will take place of . . . Well, you know the way it goes. Names, place, time.'

'Yes, I know,' Clemmie said in a stifled voice.

She still stood where he had put her when he had pushed her inside. She suddenly seemed made of stone. It's happening, she was thinking; before it was only like a play being rehearsed, now it's actually taking place.

Amber is marrying Bruce. I'm as rejected as Brown Girl. I'm as unwanted. I'm pushed out. I'm——

Then she was in Rickaby Roen's arms, in them so tightly there was not even room for thought. For a deliberate moment he held her like that, then . . . deliberately again . . . he kissed her, and it was nothing like the kiss he had given her before, the tender, gentle, comforting caress that had made her think of the father she could not remember. No, this kiss was Rickaby Roen, no one else, nothing else between. There was a savagery there, a mastery, possession. A triumph. His lips cut out everything else, cut out all the world, and where his hands touched her she seemed to burn.

'Rejected?' he said in her ear. 'Is this rejection, then?'

Once or twice she made a feeble effort to push him away, but he brushed each movement aside.

'Oh, no, Clemmie,' he told her, 'that fool I was before has had second thoughts. That's why I'm back.' He pulled her even closer.

His fingers seemed everywhere, and once Clemmie caught at them, not to push them away but guide them.

'Rickaby . . .' she said breathlessly.

He had her up in his arms now and he was moving down the hall with her. Clemmie was not protesting, instead she was listening to his heart beating close to her heart. They could have been one heart, she thought. One heart, one body, one, one one.

Then she heard the Sperry waggon labouring up the drive, and she knew that Gavin and Rachel had returned. She looked at Rickaby to see if he had heard, too, but Rickaby was putting her down and turning away. He was leaving.

With him went all the breathless wonder that had taken possession of Clemmie, that had pushed aside her misery and her rejection almost as though they never had existed.

Suddenly she was pulling out an overnight bag, cramming things into it. She knew she had to get away.

But to escape by the side door, as she still could,

would only be not to go at all. Rickaby, even if he understood her need to be alone, would be aroused at such an action, possibly follow her. Sighing, Clemmie went out to the kitchen.

'It was a great day,' Rachel was chattering. 'I've never bought such bargains. Thank you, Clem, for giving us the time off.'

'My turn next,' Clemmie claimed a little shrilly, 'so I'm leaving before it's dark. I have a flat in Brisbane, and I think if I want a successful day tomorrow it would be a good idea to go down tonight.'

Rachel looked surprised at such a sudden decision, her husband a little questioning. But both were silenced by Rickaby cutting in at once: 'Now that's what I call a sensible idea.'

Almost within minutes Clemmie was on her way to the coast, then turning north along the highway to where she had her flat, that small apartment to which she had taken Rickaby Roen one eventful night, little thinking that their lives were to keep on entangling.

But at least now she was by herself. She could think. She could take stock. She could face up to a newspaper announcement without the help of two strong encircling arms. She had to do that some time, so she would start tonight.

She pulled up at the small block, parked the Mini, went up to the top floor. It was almost dark by now, and but for the man moving from the shadow of her door and coming straight up to her, in the indistinct light Clemmie would not have seen Bruce.

'Clemmie! Oh, Clemmie!' She recognised his voice. 'Bruce! Bruce?'

'Let me come in, please, Clemmie,' he begged.

'But——'

'Please. Please!' Bruce repeated urgently.

Clemmie hesitated a moment, then unlocked the door.

They went inside.

CHAPTER SEVEN

CLEMMIE preceded Bruce into her flat, then turned to close the door after him. She found him leaning a little drunkenly against it, and, about to remonstrate with him, she noted his pallor, the strain lines round his mouth, and she saw he was fairly sober but emotionally off balance.

'What's the matter, Bruce?' she asked with concern.

'Just let me sit on a bit, Clemmie . . . be with you.'

'You can stop and rest, of course, though not for long . . . naturally not for long. Also, there are things I have to do. I don't get down to Brisbane very often these days, so I won't be sitting with you.'

'Be with me, Clemmie,' he begged.

'Bruce——'

'Be with me.' He said it so tightly that Clemmie, sensing something could snap in him, did not argue. She nodded him to a chair, wondering a little hysterically if this was becoming a custom for Clemmie Green, bringing men to her apartment to apply comfort and rest.

'I'll make coffee,' she said.

'No. No, don't go, Clemmie.'

'I'm not going, I'm making coffee.'

'Afterwards,' he begged.

'After what, Bruce?' Clemmie asked firmly.

'After I just look at you. After we talk. Oh, Clemmie, Clemmie!'

'But you did look at me at the party.' She could not stop herself from reminding that.

'Yes ... yes, the party.'

There was a moment's pause, then Clemmie said: 'Bruce, what is this all about? What are you doing here? There *is* something, isn't there?'

'Yes.'

'Then——?'

He groaned. 'Clemmie, I can't go through with it.'

'What do you mean? What are you talking about?' But she knew, of course, or at least she believed she knew. It had to be—to be—— Still, she must be *told*. *Told by Bruce.*

'I can't go through this farce with Amber,' he appealed.

'Farce?' she queried.

'Yes.'

She said bitterly, 'It didn't look like that on that night.'

'No, I know it didn't, and perhaps for a while it was as it seemed, for she is a remarkably beautiful girl.'

'The next thing you'll tell me, I suppose, is that you were carried away.'

'Yes. Trite, isn't it, but that's still what happened. She dazzled me and I fell for the old trap.'

'Except,' broke in Clemmie wisely, and wondering bitterly why she was summoning wisdom when she did not want to be wise, not, anyway, in this, 'I'm less than sure it was a trap.'

'Not a trap?'

'No.'

Bruce looked at her quickly, incredulously, he looked in complete surprise. 'A girl like Amber?'

'You,' Clemmie reminded him significantly, 'are a man like Bruce.'

'Meaning?'

'Find your own meaning.'

There was silence for a moment, then: 'All I can find, Clemmie,' Bruce said wretchedly, 'is you. I can see you and only you not just now, not just then, but all the time. Whenever I look away from Amber, and after when I'm looking at Amber, I see your face. You, you, you.'

Clemmie dug her fingernails into her palms of her hands, she steadied her lip with her teeth until it hurt.

'It's over, Bruce.'

'Oh, yes' ... bitterly ... 'I was waiting for that. First your judgment, then your recriminations. Why did I do it? Why did I fall so completely for Amber?'

'No, never that recrimination, Bruce, everyone falls for Amber.'—Except one, she remembered.

'I've given you an answer,' he reminded her. 'She dazzled me. Not only her beauty, either, but her—her——'

'Her warmth to you?' Clemmie asked shrewdly.

'So you know the old routine, Amber's routine.'

'Yes ... except that before you, Bruce, I've never seen Amber warm with anyone *in herself*.'

'What?' he demanded.

'You heard what I said.'

'Yes, but—— Oh, good lord, you're not trying to tell me it was not a well-practised line with Amber? I won't accept that. Oh, no, Clemmie, the smoke is out of my eyes' ... Rickaby's words, thought Clemmie ... 'and I'm seeing clearly again.'

'Seeing Amber's loveliness.'

'Maybe . . . but preferring yours.'

She sighed. 'I'm not lovely.'

'You are, you are, yet I, the damn fool—— Oh, Clemmie, Clemmie, it can't be too late!'

'Of course it's too late. You're being married quite soon. Is it marriage that's fretting you, Bruce? Do you enjoy the play but not the responsibility?'

'That's unfair,' he protested.

'Yet the truth?'

'No, Clemmie. I simply don't love Amber,' he said pointblank. 'When I'm beside her I have to admit I'm the proudest man alive, who wouldn't be? But I still don't love her, Clemmie. You see' . . . tensely . . . 'I can't love her. There's no love left over. Not after you.'

'Oh, Bruce!' Clemmie heard her voice make a cry of it. Too much, she was thinking, too late.

'I love you, Clemmie. I know now I loved you the first moment I saw you. You were bawling me out over Bingo's injury. I can see your dear, earnest little face.'

'Beside Amber's beautiful one?'

'Beauty is nothing.'

'It was that night you came for dinner and first met my sister.'

'Yes,' he admitted, 'one look and I was——'

'Dazzled.'

'Dazzled.' A pause. 'I can't tell you much after that, it's not very clear even to me. All I know was that everything seemed to rush past me. No, that's wrong, I really rushed, too. Things happened so quickly I lost track. I believe I lost my senses. Before I knew it there was a notice in the paper, and my parents were wiring up their intention to attend any celebration party. Then there seemed no need to wait, or so someone told me, so the final date was set. Clemmie, you must believe me when I tell you I had no part in it, not at all, it just rushed on me, as I said.'

'Yet you're still a man, aren't you? You could have said.'

'Said what? That I liked this glorious girl very much, thank you, but that I still begged to decline.'

'Bruce, you know what I mean. In this most important thing of all you surely could have made some kind of noise.'

'You'd think so, wouldn't you,' he sighed, 'but I found I had no voice.'

'... Meaning you do love her.'

'But I don't, Clemmie.'

'You may not think so now, but you must ... deep down.'

'I love you,' he insisted.

'Bruce, be sensible!' she begged.

'I'm being that. I think perhaps I'm being sensible for the first time in all my life. I love *you*, Clemmie, not Amber, and for the life of me I can't see why I should be penalised for a moment of blindness.'

'A little longer than that,' Clemmie reminded him in a stifled tone.

A minute went by in silence. Somewhere outside the building a clock chimed and Clemmie automatically counted the strokes. It was still early, she found thankfully, she would give Bruce some coffee, then send him off.

He must have read her thoughts.

'I'm not leaving, Clemmie,' he said.

She wheeled round on him.

'Of course you're leaving, Bruce, you have to leave. I'm not being your scapegoat. I'm not being your way out.'

'Oh, Clemmie, don't talk like that. I love you. *Love* you. Don't you understand? Don't you know love?'

'I thought I did,' said Clemmie.

'You did know it, and you can know it again ... with me.'

'No.'

'You can know it tonight.'

'*No!*'

'I'm not doing this for my way out, as you put it, I'm doing it because I love you, because I prefer you.'

'Prefer?' Clemmie picked that up quickly. Preference, such a pale word.

'Oh, I know everything I say is putting me in a worse light still, but Clemmie, can't you see, can't you understand, can't you realise—and accept—that it's you, not Amber. Anyway, it all would matter as much to Amber as—as——'

'You're wrong,' she said, 'it would matter a lot. Things have gone too far, she'd be embarrassed, she'd be humiliated, she'd be——'

'Who, Amber?' he half-laughed. 'Never Amber.'

'Bruce, you can't hold parties, put notices in the paper, then shrug and walk out,' Clemmie pointed out.

'Oh, I'm aware of that. But it will be Amber who does the shrugging and the walking out, I'll promise you that. Look, Clemmie, you know your sister by now ... or you should.'

'Yes, I should,' she agreed.

'Then you know how little it will really mean to her.'

Clemmie was quiet. Yes, she should know, but somehow, and she could not have said why, she did not seem to know it now. Not absolutely. Suddenly she was remembering Amber in her room that night of the engagement party, Amber seated at the dressing table staring at her lovely face, perhaps, for the first time in her life, seeing someone else's face instead. What was it Amber had said? 'I think I've even fallen for him. Me!' Had she been talking idly like she always did, or had she . . . had she . . .

'What about my stepfather?' Clemmie heard herself directing at Bruce, reminding him how such a thing as a broken engagement would never be tolerated by Daryl Coyle.

'Coyle sees me only as an eligible, nothing else. Oh, yes, I'm well aware of that. If anyone more eligible came along, it would be a different story.'

'. . . Like Rickaby Roen.' It was said before Clemmie realised it.

'What made you say that?' he asked. 'But it doesn't matter, for you do have the right trend. A richer man would suit Mr Coyle much better. Which in a way makes it better for me.'

'What do you mean?' asked Clemmie.

'That Osborne third. That very necessary monopoly on my part in Summer Heights—necessary, anyway, for Daryl Coyle. Well, Clemmie, at this stage I can't see any way I can possibly outbid Roen. So it could be my way out.'

'Way out!' Clemmie said disgustedly. 'Can't you be man enough to——'

'Oh, I'm a man all right, Clemmie.' Bruce had stood up now and he stepped across to her. He put his arms around her, and for a moment, entrapped in those arms, Clemmie knew the old magic again. But only for a moment. The grasp was not steel-tight as another grasp had been, the eyes looking into hers were not deeply, penetratingly warm as his.

'No, Bruce,' she said firmly.

'Clemmie, I'm telling you I love you.'

'And I'm telling you that you don't, not really, Bruce.'

'Then listen, darling: I love you so much I wouldn't touch you.' Bruce looked at her in longing. 'Not unless you——' His voice trailed off.

Yes, that could be love, Clemmie thought, but all at once she was remembering one heart beating where there were really two hearts, one body where there were two, one——

She pushed Bruce away. To her surprise he did not resist. He must be very tired, she thought, for the slight shove was enough to send him reeling back in the chair again.

'... Weary ...' she heard him muttering. 'Not functioning any more.'

'I'll make that coffee.' Clemmie went to the kitchen.

When she came back with the laden tray, Bruce was sprawled out on the bed, and he was deeply asleep. Oh, no, Clemmie thought, not another night sitting up!

As she sat drinking her own coffee she regarded Bruce and wondered if she could raise a laugh over the situation, for twice in a month was really making a habit of something.

But she couldn't laugh. The utter fatigue of the inert man touched her heart—always, she knew, a vulnerable heart. She simply could not waken him and show him the door.

She sat in the dark room musing on the strangeness of life. A month ago she would have given anything for this, and now ... now ...

Now she did not love Bruce, instead she loved——

No, I don't. She stopped herself sternly. I can't feel anything but contempt for that self-made, roughriding, arrogant pig. He was my way out, and that's the only reason I stayed on at Sperry, a way out just as Bruce really only wants me as a way out, but nothing else.

The room now was full of shadows. Bruce in the one bed slept on, slept perhaps, Clemmie thought, the first sleep for many nights.

After waiting an hour, she decided to shut her eyes as well. She was almost as overwrought as Bruce was, she judged, but, unlike Bruce, she prejudged she would *not* sleep.

But emotion must be a kind of panacea, for she did sleep, in fact she slept all night, and only awoke at a noise in the bed-sitter, a room still dark but showing the first light of piccaninny morning, the noise of a man moving, stretching stiffly, making a small sound of surprise at his surroundings, then looking across at Clemmie, whom he could now just see, with wonder.

'I must have died,' he groaned.

'You did, Bruce.'

'Well, thank heaven, anyway, I didn't keep you awake.' He grinned the old boyish grin that once had touched Clemmie's heart.

'Yes,' she grinned back. Then she asked boldly: 'Was that the original idea?'

'Keeping you awake?'

'Yes.'

'You and I?'

'Yes.'

'Well, yes, yet no,' he admitted. 'I did think of it, but I was a bit under the weather last night, Clemmie.'

'A little drunk,' she corrected. 'Don't apologise, Bruce, nothing was taken down to be used against you.'

'What a girl! But you're not entirely on the right track. I do remember, and I did mean what I said.'

'What you *think* you said. You weren't really there, remember.'

'Yes, but I said——'

'Think you said,' she corrected.

'Clemmie——'

'Bruce, she's lovely, Amber is very lovely, and she's something any man would want, every man, *but you've got her.*'

'Clemmie——' he began.

'Also, do you know this?' she went on. 'When you're beside her you know something you could never know with anyone else.'

'But——'

'And, Bruce' . . . a pause . . . 'she loves you.'

'Amber does?'

'She *loves* you, Bruce.' Clemmie said it truly now. For Amber did love him, and her sister knew it positively in that moment—a light love, perhaps, but such a love would be all that Amber was capable of, would ask in return, but she still loved him.

'Amber loves me.' Bruce was staring at Clemmie in surprise . . . also in something else.

But Clemmie was not waiting for any more soul-barings, she had had enough.

'You're going,' she said firmly, 'and at once.'

'Yes, Clemmie.'

'And Bruce——'

'Yes, Clemmie?'

'You were never here last night.'

'You mean——'

'Yes,' she said firmly.

'And this morning?' He actually managed another grin at her.

'You were never here at all.'

'No, Clemmie. Thank you, Clemmie. Clemmie, you're wonderful—you must at least let me tell you that.'

'I'll think you're wonderful if you go quietly down the stairs and out of the apartment without any telling, Bruce.'

'Then I'll do that.' He made a few steps to the door, then came back and kissed her.

Then he went.

Clemmie checked through the window and saw Bruce unlock his car and move off. She took no notice of two other vehicles parked in the same area, tenants' no doubt.

But the cars were not together, and it was Rickaby Roen's that sparked to life first, that moved away before the other.

Daryl Coyle moved more slowly, for the man at the wheel was older; also he was deep in thought. They were unpleasant thoughts, angry thoughts. Daryl Coyle drove down the highway for some miles, drove broodingly, resentfully, then suddenly, even a little violently for such a well-regulated man, he turned back again.

But Rickaby Roen had changed his course long before Coyle, indeed he had only gone a hundred yards before he returned. He ran up the apartment steps and knocked on Clemmie's door. The knock startled Clemmie. After she had seen Bruce's car move off, she had crossed to the door and locked it. Then, all at once savouring the emptiness of her apartment, she had leaned against the door, looking gratefully around the void, no one here but herself. For a few moments she had remained there, putting thoughts aside, simply being alone and enjoying it.

The knock was so imperative she almost sprang to action. The firmness of it, she fumed, was almost as punitive as a hard hand across her back. Angrily, she turned and unlocked the door again, then stood staring at Rickaby.

'You!' she gasped.

'Was it another client you were expecting?' He was striding boldly in.

'Client?' she questioned.

'You know what I mean.'

'I don't, but I dislike what I think you could mean.'

'Then dislike it, because I mean it. No, none of that. If I remember you tried that once before.' He had caught the hand she instinctively had raised before she could use it on him. Perhaps she wouldn't have used it, she did not know, but she did know she had never felt so furiously angry in all her life.

'I take it,' she said, only keeping her voice steady with a hard effort, 'you're speaking of Bruce.'

'Bruce?' he questioned.

'Bruce Malling.'

'So he was the client,' Rickaby drawled.

'As though you didn't know!' she said furiously. 'How long have you been waiting outside to make sure?'

'Yes,' Rickaby almost yawned, 'I did know. But I haven't been waiting long. Now are you answered?'

'I'm not answered,' she retorted. 'Why are you here at all?'

'*You* ask that?' His brows had raised. 'To finish what you started at Sperry, of course.'

'I—I did not!'

'No? Then you could have fooled me. However, after a night with Malling ... no, lady, *put that hand down.*'

'You're hateful!' she hit out.

'But true.'

'Untrue,' Clemmie insisted. 'There was nothing.'

'He stayed the night?'

'He was waiting when I arrived.'

'*He stayed the night?*' Rickaby repeated.

'Yes. Only it wasn't like that.'

'I'm all ears, if not all credulity,' he shrugged.

'I have no reason to tell you,' Clemmie said wearily. 'But just to close this whole distasteful thing——'

'Oh, not distasteful to you, surely?' he drawled.

'I'll tell you,' she ignored. 'It was' ... a hunch of slim shoulders ... 'just as you said.'

'Yes, madam?'

'The smoke got out of his eyes.'

'Malling's brown orbs?'

'They're russet,' she corrected.

'So now they're not Amber-inflamed any more.'

'How cruel you can be!' Clemmie said bitterly.

He shrugged. 'Then I'll put it this way: He's now undazzled.'

'No one is ever completely undazzled with Amber. No, he's—Bruce is——'

'Back with his first love.'

'I wasn't that,' she sighed.

'... But wish you were?'

Clemmie stuck out her chin. 'Yes ... yes, I was. Oh, why are you questioning me like this?'

'Because I have to have some data, I have to have something to go on with. Am I to gather then that the eligible Bruce Malling is having second thoughts on things?'

'No. Not after what I told him.'

'You told him?'

'Yes.'

He looked at her keenly. 'And that was?'

'That Amber loved him.'

'Now that was a sacrificial whimsy on your part,' he jeered.

'Except that it wasn't a whimsy. You see, in her way, I believe she does.'

'In her way?'

'There are many ways,' Clemmie insisted.

'So Malling weakened?'

'Well, not exactly, but he did go.'

'So,' was all Rickaby replied.

A silence fell between them.

As though he had done it all his life, Rickaby crossed to the small kitchen and made two cups of coffee. After he had brought them back and handed Clemmie hers, he did not speak for several minutes.

Then he said: 'Are you an expert liar or a simpleton, Clementine?'

She looked at him in inquiry.

'To expect me to believe this or to tell it in all innocence?'

'What I've told you is true,' she persisted.

'You're giving Amber back her feller?'

'If you want it put that way——'

'I do.'

'Then yes,' she said.

'Is it a grand gesture, or don't you want him any more?'

That was not easy to answer, and Clemmie avoided it by saying: 'Anyway, if Bruce is going to marry Amber it had to be done at once. If he's beaten to the Osborne third, which' ... a direct look at Rickaby ... 'could happen, I know my stepfather might have second thoughts.'

'For your sister?'

'Yes. He's always wanted ... no, demanded ... the top for Amber. I never knew why.'

'No?' Rickaby said, and his tone was dry.

'No.' Clemmie shook her head.

'Not even hazarded a guess?'

Clemmie looked at him. 'What are you talking about?'

He only shrugged.

Presently he mused: 'And you think that Bruce Malling mightn't add up high enough?'

'How could he when you propose to outbid him for Osborne's third, making Bruce still only one-third to your two-thirds, making you the boss.'

'I'm always the boss,' Rickaby shrugged.

'And always the roughrider,' she added.

'Have I been to you?' he asked.

'Yes, your sort always is. You're the ruthless, overbearing, overriding——'

'All right!' He held up a hand. 'You've made your point.'

'Have you taken it?' Clemmie asked.

'Part of it. I've accepted the fact ... or so you say ... that Malling only hotfooted it here to cry on your shoulder, that you've duly smoothed and soothed and now he will return to Amber's side and overyone will live happily ever after.'

'Not everyone,' Clemmie said impulsively; not even aware she was speaking.

But she was aware the next moment. The man had drawn her to him and his eyes were burning down into hers.

'*Not* everyone? You mean—not you?'

'Yes—no——I don't know.'

'Then if you're not unhappy about Malling, as you have said, then you must be unhappy about someone else. Clemmie, tell me.'

'I can't—I don't know. You're hurting me! I only want——' She only wanted those two to be happy, was what she started to say, but somehow the words would not come. I only want—Rickaby. She heard herself speaking that deep down inside her, she heard . . . and she tightened her lips.

'I don't know what I want,' she said miserably at last.

'And I don't, either,' he said bitterly, 'but I think you should start to find out, assess the position, because I believe you're going to have a third visitor to this flat. While I waited, someone else waited.'

'Someone else?' she queried.

'Your stepfather, Daryl Coyle—oh, yes, it was him. I've never met him, but I make it my business to check these kind of things, recognise a face.'

'But why?' asked Clemmie, perplexed. 'Why should Daryl want me?'

'Wanted for questioning.' Rickaby laughed. 'What have you been doing? No, don't tell me, I know, you've been stealing his favourite daughter's beau.'

'I haven't!'

'Well, spending the night with him, which is worse. Well, this time it's all yours, Clemmie, you have to wriggle out of it yourself.'

'But why was Stepfather out there?' she persisted. 'Surely he can't think——'

'I don't know how his brain works, and I'm not sure if I want to find out. But I'm sure, although I saw him come out of the parking lot, that he'll be back. Clemmie——'

She looked at him wrechedly.

'I wish I could help you, Clemmie. I can't. But don't let him hurt you, promise me that, and when it's all over——'

'What's all over?'

Rickaby shrugged. 'When it's over come back to Sperry to be kissed and mopped up.'

'Mopped up and kissed,' Clemmie corrected a little stupidly, 'you have the wrong order. Rickaby, why? Why would I have need to be—to be soothed? Rickaby——' But she spoke to nothing. Taking advantage of her distress, Rickaby had left.

Half an hour went past before there was another knock, and Clemmie was just beginning to think that Rickaby had been playing the fool when he had said what he had, when it happened. The clanger clanged. Full of foreboding, she answered the summons, and yes, Rickaby was right. Daryl Coyle stood there.

For the first time in Clemmie's memory, and that was a good part of her life, Daryl Coyle seemed not quite sure of himself.

He had always comprised the perfect human iceberg to her, showing above surface a remarkably handsome, completely controlled, composed man, barely suggesting the depths ... ice-cold, of course ... he had beneath. But now he had emerged, and the good looks were a little frayed, the self-discipline rather tattered. Why, he seemed almost old, Clemmie thought, and he appeared agitated. He tried to hide the agitation, but it still showed clearly.

At once, as though her thoughts had reached him, he straightened himself, became the suave gentleman again, no sign of emotion. He even managed a bland smile when Clemmie said: 'Stepfather, why are you here?'

'My dear,' he said as smoothly as ever, 'can I not visit my stepdaughter without being questioned about it?'

'I'm sorry. Come in.' Clemmie stepped aside, and Daryl entered. He looked sharply around him as he crossed the threshold, his piercing eyes searching for something, but Clemmie, behind him, did not see the look.

Unlike her previous visitor, Daryl did not come to the point at once. Instead he seated himself in the chair Clemmie indicated and said yes, a cup of tea would be welcome.

Clemmie had not suggested it, for she had not long finished Rickaby's coffee, but she put on the kettle, and Daryl spoke pleasantly to her from the bed-sit as she did so.

'A charming little place, Clementine.'

'Yes.'

'I should have called before, child, but you know how it is.'

Clemmie didn't, but she agreed.

So handy to town ... such a nice area ... she heard his voice go on and on, and she wondered what was the real trend.

She did not have long to wait. When she brought in the tray she could see that the veneer was wearing thin. There were anxious lines on Daryl Coyle's face, lines she had never noticed before, and she saw that he was clenching his hands, then, remembering where he was, unclenching them. When they were clenched, the knucklebones stood up white and prominent. Undoubtedly he was under strain.

It only needed Clemmie's faltered: 'Stepfather?' to break the floodgates.

Mr Coyle put his cup down and said abruptly:

'He was here, wasn't he?'

'Who?'

'Oh, don't play around, Clementine, give me the truth. It's no use lying, I saw him.'

'Then if you saw whoever you're talking about there's no need for me to answer you.'

'Nonetheless I want an answer. Was—Bruce Malling here last night?'

'If you saw him——'

'*Was* he?' he repeated.

'Yes,' said Clemmie, 'he was.'

She watched in amazement as the man got up from the chair and crossed to the window, she listened in disbelief at his angry tattoo of tight fists on the window. Why, he was almost out of control of himself. He was standing in profile, and something about his finely chiselled features grabbed at her. Where had she seen . . . whom had she seen . . .

Daryl was coming back to the chair.

'I didn't follow him here,' he said, 'I had no reason to believe that he would—that he——' He bit hard on his lip. 'No, I came to tell you that your aunt's will has finally been wound up, or near enough to it, but we'll leave that till later. What I want to know is——'

'Yes?'

'Was it the first time?'

'The first time Bruce has come here?' she asked.

'The first time that he and you——'

'Yes?' Clemmie asked again, but this time more tightly.

'You know what I mean!' he fairly hissed at her.

'I think I can guess. And the answer is neither no or yes. I think you are asking me if Bruce and I sleep together' ... she saw his lips tighten ... 'so I can't say yes, it's the first time, or no, it's not the first time, because we haven't, not in the past, most certainly we won't in the future, and, for your present information, not last night.'

'Then what in heaven and earth *did* you do last night?'

As Clemmie stared at him in undisguised distaste, Daryl Coyle must have decided to change his tactics. He altered his face, he unclenched his hands.

'Clementine, I want you to be absolutely honest with me. I won't blame you, my dear, you're young, and I can remember my own youth.'

'Please go on,' Clemmie said frozenly.

'I want you to tell me if what you've just said is true. I want you to tell me *regardless*.'

'That Bruce and I were never lovers?' Against his will once more that instinctive moue of distaste on her stepfather's part, but still Clemmie continued.

'We were not,' she said. '*Not*. Do you want me to sign a declaration? Do you want me to open the window and tell the world?' The window. His face in profile. The chiselled features. Where? Who?

'No. No, of course not. Of course I believe you. But

why did he come here? Why, Clementine?'

'I don't know,' she sighed.

'You must know. A man doesn't stay all night unless he——'

'Yes?'

'Unless he's in love.'

'He *is* in love,' she told him. 'With Amber.'

'I thought so. I believed so. She thinks and believes so. But——' Once again Daryl crossed to the window to beat a tattoo. Once again Clemmie frowned over that proud profile.

Then——

Her astonished gasp brought him back into the room. He looked down on Clemmie and she looked incredulously back, looked at her stepfather.

'I never knew ... I never guessed ... not at any time did I dream ...'

He waited. He waited a long time, then, when he saw she was still word-robbed with shock, he said the words for her. No, one word. One name.

'Amber?'

'Yes.' Now Clemmie's tongue was working again. She whispered : 'You—she——'

'Yes, I'm her father. So now you know, Clementine, how I would understand if anything happened last night. I would understand, because once it was like that with me.'

'I can't ever imagine——' Clemmie stopped herself. She had been going to say : 'I can't ever imagine anything like that of you.'

'You'll understand, too,' Daryl Coyle continued, 'how I'm so desperately anxious for Amber now ... how I've always been anxious.'

'Yes,' Clemmie understood, 'because you love her.'

'A father does love his child.'

A silence for a while, then:

'Does she know?' Clemmie asked.

'Know?'

'Does Amber know you're her father?'

'We've never spoken of it, but I think Amber, being Amber, being intelligent, being——' He paused, and Clemmie knew he was thinking: '... being my daughter, she would.'

'My mother is Amber's mother, too?' she asked presently.

'Of course. Alison was my first and only dear love. I think I'd better tell you, Clementine.'

'Yes, I think so,' Clemmie said.

'We were very much in love, Alison and I, but we were also very young, and I was not established, something that meant a great deal to me. Besides wanting to be a success, I wanted everything for Alison, and that was why I put marriage aside until I could give her what I felt she must have.

'But she was not in agreement. She was not so complacent then' ... a remembering smile ... 'but I still held out and insisted on waiting, fool that I was, and I went overseas.'

'Telling Mother you would come back?'

'I did come back.'

'But too late,' she said.

Now an acid note crept into Daryl Coyle's rich voice. 'She didn't wait,' he said. 'To spite me——'

'To spite you?'

'*To spite me* she married your father. He was much older than she was, he—well, we'll leave that, shall we?'

Clemmie stood very still, she stood almost stiffly.

'Go on,' she said again.

'When I returned she had had you. I never intended to start things again, she never did, neither of us are people like that, but it still happened, Clementine. Then—the accident happened.'

'Father's accident?'

'Yes.'

'Was it?' she asked flatly.

'Was it what, Clementine?'

'Was it an accident? I mean, he was a good swimmer —Aunt Mary always told me that. Yet an able swimmer brings his small daughter safely to a bank, then— then—— Was it an accident, Daryl?'

'I don't know, but it must have been, it had to be. No one knew but us. In a way perhaps it was better. No one' ... in pride ... 'could have accepted Amber as your father's daughter.'

'No,' Clemmie said. Presently she spoke again, spoke dully.

'So he died.'

'There was never any public question about the tragedy, it was purely accidental, I believe that, and you must, too.'

'But you just answered me that you didn't know.'

'I added that it must have been, that it had to be. No, Clementine, it was simply and sadly one of those things.'

'Yes,' said Clemmie bitterly, 'one of those things.'

Another silence.

'Poor child,' Daryl sympathised, 'it's a wonder to me that you've never guessed before.'

She sighed. 'No, I never guessed.'

'Well, it's all water under the bridge now, there's no going back.'

'And you wouldn't want to go back.'

'I love Amber next to Alison, and believe me, Clementine, there are no limits to me to either love. That was why, when I came here last night to tell you that the estate was winding up and I saw Malling's car that I thought—well, I thought——'

'Of your own youth.'

'Well—yes. I looked back and remembered the sudden fierce longing in a man, the——'

'I understand,' Clemmie broke in coldly. 'How did you know to come to the flat?'

'I didn't. I took a chance.'

'As Bruce did.'

He winced at that, but tried to hide it. 'And you've told me the truth, my dear?'

'I have,' she said, 'but would it have mattered if I hadn't? Would it have been such a terrible thing if for once Bruce——'

'For Amber, yes. Everything must be perfect for Amber. I know I can't expect you to understand that, but——'

'I still understand,' Clemmie said.

Before he could question her again, she added: 'There was nothing. Nothing. All we did was sit and talk. I believe Bruce was a little fagged out socially ... you've been driving him rather hard, I think. Also, if you don't allow for that, allow at least for a man's irresistible urge to get away from it all for a while, remind yourself how *you* left the fold, the fold of Alison's arms' ... a pause ... 'tell yourself that history is only repeating itself.' A tilt of her chin. 'And why not?'

'But—but—Amber?'

'In your time it was Alison,' she reminded him.

'I only left to better myself.'

'So did Bruce. He came to me solely to talk of his future.' Well, that was the truth, Clemmie thought.

Daryl was looking at her curiously. 'I can see I've always underestimated you, Clementine, you are quite a remarkably astute person. But what puzzles me still is your generosity. You had a wonderful chance last night to——'

'To take a man away from the woman he loves?' Clemmie asked.

There was a long silence this time, but not one of distaste. Instead Daryl Coyle said carefully, hopefully:

'. . . Does he? Does Bruce love Amber?'

Clemmie did not let a moment go by. She said:

'Yes. *Yes*.'

'Then thank heaven. Thank heaven! Because my girl, my little sweet girl, really loves him. Incredulous, isn't it, how she follows me? Restraint in everything, always her own mistress as I was my own master, yet for one man, just as it was for me for one woman, no restraint, aloofness no more.'

'I think by that you mean Amber loves Bruce,' said Clemmie drily.

'Oh, yes!'

'Then' . . . and Clemmie got up . . . 'that's enough.'

Daryl had got up, too. Presently he said: 'The wedding is on Saturday. Will you be there?'

'No, I'll be back at work.'

'That's a pity.' He began brushing down his suit. 'Clementine, you won't . . . you wouldn't . . .'

'Yes, Stepfather?'

'You wouldn't ever mention what happened last night?'

'What didn't happen, you mean,' she corrected. 'No, I won't.'

'Then thank you, thank you, Clementine. By the way, you never said where you worked.'

'Neither you nor Mother asked,' she pointed out.

'No, and we're sorry about that, but you know how it is ... Is it a stud?'

'Yes. An old one still functioning under its original name—Sperry.'

'Interesting,' said Daryl, patently uninterested. 'Well, my dear, I must go. Do I look as though——'

'You've undergone an all-night vigil? No, Stepfather, you're as impeccable as ever. What will your explanation be?'

'Explanation?' he queried.

'Your absence last night.'

'I never explain,' he reminded her proudly. He stepped forward and took her hand. Then he actually, and much to Clemmie's discomfort, kissed her brow.

He went at once, and Clemmie immediately turned the key in the door. She wanted no more visitors. Three, she thought exhaustedly, had been more than enough.

She crossed to the single bed and lay down. She thought about a lot of things, but most of all of a man she could not remember who had swum ashore with a little girl, then ... then ... she began to sob. She was exhausted when sleep finally saved her.

She slept well into the afternoon.

CHAPTER EIGHT

CLEMMIE lay without moving for some minutes before she dragged herself up. Although the sleep had released her, it had not refreshed her. She still felt exhausted after the most momentous day ... and a night before the day ... she had ever experienced. Even now she could not credit that what had happened had actually taken place, that three men had come here, all with different purposes: Bruce in search of escape, or escape was what he had thought, Daryl Coyle for her reassurance, and Rickaby Roen——

But Clemmie found she could not examine that.

She forced herself out to the small kitchen and brewed a strong coffee. By now the first shadows of dusk were stealing into the room, and she knew that any shopping would be out of the question, that the stores would be closed by the time she reached them. Anyway, she did not need anything, it had only been an excuse for her absence to offer to Rachel.

She decided to go home to Sperry ... Clemmie paused a moment, realising she had said 'home'. She felt she could not bear another night in the flat. Rachel would be surprised to see no purchases after all the bundles she herself had brought back, but Clemmie knew she would overcome that.

She felt better after she had reached this decision, and even managed to eat a slice of bread and cheese. She would probably need that small sustenance, she had only once travelled the hinterland road at night and then had finished up in a ditch.

However, she did not let this experience deter her. She drained the coffee, rinsed the mug, took up the overnight bag she had not even opened, then went out and locked the door after her. Downstairs Miss Muffett awaited, and within minutes she was on the road.

She was all right on the brightly lit highway, and all right, too, for some time afterwards, for a tatter of day still persisted, and several lights extended beyond the town mile.

But by the time she reached the lesser turn-off that led to Sperry it was quite dark, and after a few kilometres the illumination was cancelled entirely. Why not, Clemmie accepted, there would only be a handful of people out here to be serviced. She slackened speed and began to concentrate on her driving. Star shadows on mountain curves could be disastrous. Thank goodness the traffic was non-existent.

Yet was it? On her third mountain a powerful beam halted her with its blinding brilliance. Clemmie slammed on her brakes and crept into a convenient corner with the intention of letting the very ignorant motorist, or so she considered, pass. No one should drive through these steep hills with full lights like this.

But this car was not driving through, it was pulling up. Pulling up not far from Clemmie. Alarmed, Clemmie was out of Miss Muffett in a second and running away ... at least away she thought, but actually running into someone instead. Someone who had got out of the brilliantly lit car intentionally to intercept her, that was very apparent, and Clemmie remembered several unpleasant incidents in the hinterland at night. She made a fresh spurt, but it was too late. Two arms had caught her.

'So——' drawled a voice Clemmie recognised. She had no need to look up to murmur:

'You again!'

'If "you" in that tone of voice means me, yes,' Rickaby Roen said enigmatically.

'It does. Do you always travel with such blinding lights? And do you always pull up and chase the other car's driver?'

'Yes,' he said obligingly, obliging Clemmie with one answer, since obviously she looked beyond coping with two replies even though she had asked a question twice.

He tacked on: 'I knew it would be you.'

'How could you know?'

'How does spring know when to burst?' he answered lightly, yet somewhere in the lightness was a deeper tone, something she had noticed before in Rickaby's replies.

'Don't be absurd!' she said crossly.

'I wasn't being. I was telling the truth. I simply knew it would be you.'

'You couldn't have known I would come back to-night.'

'I knew,' Rickaby declared. 'I even knew the time. After Daryl Coyle departs, I told myself, she'll be so exhausted she'll fall into her bed. She'll sleep into late afternoon, then decide to come home.'

'It isn't home,' she objected.

'Yet you've come.'

She could not deny that, so she mumbled stubbornly: 'I still could have stayed over. Shopped. I know Rachel at least will expect parcels.'

'Ah, I even thought of that.' He grinned. 'I have some likely boxes in my car. You can carry those in and satisfy Rachel.'

'I'll do nothing of the sort—I mean, Rachel would only wonder at empty arms, but she'd never be nosey.'

'Everyone is nosey,' he assured her. 'I'm anxious, for instance, to know what Daryl Coyle came about.'

'It could have been for nothing in particular,' Clemmie snapped. 'It could have been a social call. I am, after all, his stepdaughter.'

'Only it wasn't,' he said shrewdly.

'It was—at first,' Clemmie retorted.

'I think you mean before he saw Bruce go in.'

'Yes,' she had to admit.

'You mean' ... a disbelieving smile ... 'prior to that he merely came to say howdy, stepdaughter.'

'Well, not exactly,' she confessed. 'Not Daryl.'

'Then?'

'He came to tell me that Aunt Mary's will had gone through,' Clemmie supplied. This man would get it out of her some time, so why not at once?

'Ah, yes, the will. So the cogs of the law have finished grinding.'

'Yes. Well—almost.'

'And you are now an heiress, or near-heiress?'

'I told you before, I'm nothing of the sort.'

'Did you?' He showed a marked lack of interest in her inheritance, or lack of it. He even yawned.

'Aunt Mary, with my agreement, was leaving everything to her only brother's wife, to Mother, to her sister-in-law Alison. Is that explicit enough?'

'It is. Thank you. And the agreement, of course, would please friend Coyle.'

'Oh, it did,' she assured him.

'... But in spite of your generous acceptance did it really please you?'

'I wanted it that way,' said Clemmie. 'I needed no material memory of Aunt Mary, and anyhow, there was the musical box.'

'Come again?'

Clemmie sighed but complied. 'It played *Winter Wonderland*, and its tinkling, frosty, icicle notes on a hot Queensland day always fascinated me.'

'Perhaps you loved it because you loved her,' Rickaby suggested.

'Perhaps,' Clemmie agreed softly.

'Perhaps you would be the same with anyone you loved.' He was looking at her closely, his expression enigmatical.

'You mean accept a musical box instead of money?' she asked deliberately.

'You know I didn't mean that, though how you came to agree to such a poor inheritance I'll never know.'

'If I remember, I even suggested it,' she said.

'Yes,' Rickaby nodded, 'that would be you. But leaving musical boxes and coming to love——'

'No, thank you. I want to go home.'

'Home?' He lifted one brow.

'Sperry.'

'You're almost there. Can you follow me in your car, or would you prefer to leave it here and ride with me? No, no need to answer. You'll be independent, of course, and drive.'

'Of course,' Clemmie agreed. She turned and went back to the Mini.

When they reached Sperry, Clemmie managed to

get to her room with only a minimum of chatter from Rachel.

'Town's exciting,' Rachel babbled, 'but it's good to get back, isn't it? I see you have more sales resistance than I have, Clem. Gavin will no doubt have something to say to me about that. You look tired, though, dear. Pop into bed and I'll send Rickaby in with some hot milk.'

When Rickaby came, Clemmie kept her eyes tightly closed until he had gone out again. Then she took the milk and poured it out of the window. It was not until she came back to her bed and her bedside table that she noticed the note he had written.

It said briefly: 'Strictly for human consumption. No additives.'

Clemmie sighed. She could have done with a hot, untampered-with nightcap.

She slept, though, and was out the next morning as early as the rest of them. Now that their stock had grown there was plenty to do, and Clemmie was busy grooming when Rickaby strolled up.

'Does that have to be done every day?' he asked in genuine surprise.

'I thought you'd once lived on a farm?' she commented.

'Not one with four feet.'

'Well, you comb your hair regularly, don't you?'

'I believed animals used wind combs.'

'Wild ones might, but this fellow's no brumby.' Clemmie rested her dark head against the horse's mane.

Rickaby watched for a while, then he said:

'You love all this, don't you?'

'Yes, I like it very much.'

'... Too much to give it up?'

'Give it up?'

'For the man you love.'

'I don't love any man,' she said firmly.

'What about Bruce Malling?'

'He goes in for promotions,' she said, 'not studs.'

'You haven't answered my question. I asked——'

'I know what you asked, and I thought all this was finished before.'

'So did I, Clemmie, but somehow now I'm not so sure.'

'Mr Roen, what is all this?' Clemmie demanded.

'Us, to be honest. Us, when we're married. You see, there won't be this.' He looked around him and nodded.

'We're not being married,' she insisted.

'Oh, yes, we are. The only barrier previously was Bruce, but now that you no longer love him——' He looked at her and waited.

'I never said that, I said that it was past, over.'

'Perhaps, but I challenge you to say you still do.'

Clemmie was silent.

'See?' he smiled.

After a few minutes of intense combing, Clemmie mumbled: 'We're still not being married.'

'You and Bruce?'

'You and—I. But will you tell me this, that if we did——'

'Yes?'

'Then where would my giving up the stud come in? You're not thinking of giving it up, are you?'

'Oh, no, I believe I like it almost as much as you do, but I'm a business man, and as such have to be away a lot.'

'Well?'

'Well, I'm not the kind of business man who leaves his wife behind him. *Now* do you understand?'

'No,' said Clemmie.

'Then think it over. You might even change your mind when you go to your sister's wedding. There's nothing, I've been told, like weddings to give ideas.'

'I wasn't asked,' she said. 'I mean not officially.'

'But your attendance would be taken for granted, of course.'

'There's no "of course", not in our family.' Our 'family'! Clemmie stood silent a moment. 'Rickaby—Mr Roen——' she burst out.

'Rickaby.'

'Did you know . . . have you ever noticed . . . guessed . . . my stepfather . . .'

'Yes, of course,' he said simply. 'Haven't you?'

'You don't know what I'm talking about.'

'I do,' he assured her. 'Last night, and this is what I think you're asking, it came to you for the first time that you and your sister are—half-sisters. Am I right?'

'Yes. But——'

'But how could I tell? Use your sense.'

'Sense?' she queried.

'Amber's resemblance to Coyle.'

'I'd never seen the resemblance before,' she confessed.

'Those close seldom do, and by close I mean living close, growing up together. Did' . . . with a sudden fierce tightness . . . 'that damn fellow suddenly tell you?'

'No, he didn't. He was standing near the window and all at once it became clear to me. So I asked.'

'And he couldn't deny it?'

'He was proud of it,' she said.

A few moments went by. Then:

'You poor kid!' Rickaby came round and took the brushes out of Clemmie's hands, put them on the ground. He placed his arms around her. 'Cry,' he ordered.

'I cried it all out yesterday, I'm dry now. I cried away—Dad. You see, I couldn't help wondering if he —did he—could he——'

'I know, I know.' He patted Clemmie's shoulder. 'I know, little one.'

'Then do you think——'

'I don't know that. None of us know. The best thing is to think not.'

'But if I can't?' she asked piteously.

'You must make yourself, make yourself realise that it's now all over. Over, Clementine.' He tilted her chin and narrowed his eyes on her. 'Over,' he said again.

'How can I do that?' she sighed.

'By turning the page and reading the next page, your own page instead. Determine what it is ... *who* it is ... you want. Because, for all the glib answers you tell me you gave to Bruce Malling——'

'I did give them.'

'I'm still not sure of your answer *to yourself*. Forget being heroic, Clemmie, heroic to Amber, if there's anything still in you ... for Bruce ... admit it now. Take it now.'

'I——'

'It's your life,' he said, and he turned and walked off.

It was not discussed any more that day, nor on the following morning. If Clemmie had not been so busy on the thousand and one things that have to be done in a stud, even a minor stud like Sperry, the grooming, the feeding, the exercising, the stable routine, she would have brooded over Rickaby's silence. She did not want to be silent herself, she was brimming over with words, but they were chaotic, confused words, not always understood even by Clemmie herself. Of course I want Bruce for Amber, she told herself a dozen times, of course I want Amber for Bruce. But somewhere, unbidden, uninvited, always there stirred that small wonder, that unsureness. I'm waiting for something to happen, Clemmie knew, some indication, I'm willing it to prompt me. What, I don't know, but I'm looking for an indication.

It came at lunch with a ring on the phone.

Rickaby took it. Presently he put the phone down and came to Clemmie.

'It's for you—your stepfather. So you told him where you were.'

'I said Sperry,' she told him.

'But not for whom you worked?'

'No. Nothing intentional. He simply wasn't interested.'

'He is now,' said Rickaby. 'I naturally announced myself.'

'Oh! What does he want?'

'I suggest you find out,' Rickaby shrugged.

Daryl Coyle's rich voice came over the wire as bland and self-assured as ever. It was hard to recall that only a short time ago this sophisticated, suave man had thrown himself on Clemmie's mercy, or at least reached desperately out for what she could tell him.

'My dear,' he began, 'you didn't tell me where you were working.'

'I said Sperry.'

'But not Roen's Sperry. I believe Roen was the name that was just announced.'

'Yes. Rickaby Roen.' Before her stepfather could break in, Clemmie added: 'The same person for whom Amber once worked.'

'And the same person now interested in our Summer Heights Estate.'

'I only work for Mr Roen's stud, so I wouldn't know that,' she said.

'Of course. A coincidence, though.' A pause, and then warmly, enthusiastically, if Daryl Coyle could be either warm or enthusiastic:

'Clementine, dear, we want you to come over.'

'For the wedding?'

'Certainly for the wedding, indeed, Amber has an idea she would like you for her bridesmaid. She is, after all, your sister.'

'Half-sister.' But Clemmie said it to herself.

'I would like you before that on my own accord, to —well, there are certain details to be gone over.'

'The will?' she queried.

'The will is among the details, yes.'

'But I only inherit a musical box, remember.'

'My dear!'—'My dear' again?—'My dear, do come as soon as you can. I'm sure Mr Roen could spare you for a while.'

'I don't know,' said Clemmie. 'I haven't been in his employ all that long.'

'On a special occasion like this?'

'I suppose so. Yes, I'll come.'

When Clemmie put down the phone, Rickaby was not there.

'He went off quite abruptly,' provided a puzzled

Rachel, obviously confused at girls who go shopping and come back with nothing, at bosses who suddenly depart, 'but he said to tell you to go if you liked. Do you understand that?' Rachel looked as though she didn't.

'Yes,' Clemmie told her. 'It means I'll be away another night.'

Rachel looked more confused than ever, but she came to the door, after Clemmie had repacked her overnight bag, to wave her off.

Clemmie was at Summer Heights Estate some two hours later, she was even sitting in Stepfather's office. His girls, he said proudly, his Alison and Amber, were down the coast shopping.

He poured two sherries and handed one to Clemmie, something he had never done before, and Clemmie held the goblet tightly, wondering what was to come.

'Apart from the wedding' ... there was the slightest flick of a frown on Daryl's well-preserved, extremely good-looking face, but it was gone almost at once, 'I have something else to ask you, Clementine.'

'You asked it before,' Clemmie reminded him, 'and I said that anything discussed that night would never be discussed with anyone again.'

'Not that.' Daryl looked surprised that Clemmie had found need even to remind him of the episode. 'No, it's your father's sister's will.'

'Aunt Mary's will?'

'Yes.'

'No need to be distressed, Stepfather,' she said. 'I know, and I told you I knew long ago, what I'm to receive.'

'A sentimental memento.'

'Yes.'

'Of course, and that's all, Clementine, except—
well——'

'Except?' Clemmie looked at her stepfather in surprise. Surely he was not going to offer her more than
the musical box, though perhaps for all his high-
handedness he was still feeling indebted to her, grateful for what she had assured him, or perhaps her
mother——

No, she soon learned that it was not that. There
was something more for her, but it was not inspired
by either her stepfather or her mother, it was Aunt
Mary's own hand reaching to Clemmie beyond death.

'Although all the money was left to Alison,' Daryl
was explaining in a low voice, 'there was a codicil, a—
well, a very unusual one.'

'Yes?'

'It was to be your right to claim, if you decided to
claim, and that claim' ... his voice even lower ... 'to
be accepted. Really, it was most distasteful of Mary to
add that codicil. She must have known that the care of
you, dear Clementine, would be as near to our hearts
as—well——' He smiled winningly at Clemmie and
held up his glass to her. 'You're very precious to us,
Clementine,' he intoned.

'How much money could I claim?' Clemmie asked.

He told her, and it was substantial. Aunt Mary's
brand of writing must have been much more profit-
able than any of them had thought.

'Yes, I'm *very* precious to you.' Clemmie could
not resist that.

Presently she said: 'But Amber should have
enough money, surely—I mean, presumably she'll be
helped by' ... a pause ... 'her parents.' Clemmie
succeeded in keeping her voice emotionally detached.

'And will need every cent of any help for Bruce.'

'For Bruce?' she echoed.

'Bruce is going to move at last,' Daryl told her. 'He's going to make an offer for Osborne's third before Roen does, assure himself of the two-thirds he must have of the estate. Ordinarily I would have no fears, not with the Malling family backing, but this fellow, this Roen, appears to be a veritable Midas. Is he really as well placed as I've heard?'

'I only strap for him,' said Clemmie. 'I'm not his accountant.'

'But more goes on than strapping,' Daryl insinuated slyly, 'a youngish man like Roen, a nice-looking girl like you.'

'Nothing else goes on,' said Clemmie stonily. 'I'm a strapper, nothing else. I've never been a femme fatale like Amber.'

'It takes all sorts,' Daryl said pleasantly, 'and you must believe me when I assure you that you're very attractive in your way. —Perhaps, too, in Roen's way?'

'Do you want me to ask him?' she snapped.

'Dear child!' Daryl let the reproof sink in, or sink in, he hoped, for presently he said persuasively: 'If you could find out if he really intends to bid.'

'Oh, he does intend that,' she said.

'He's actually said so?'

'Yes.'

'How much?'

'He's very rich,' Clemmie pointed out.

'I know.' A sigh from Daryl Coyle. 'That's why I'm hoping that what your aunt has offered you will be— well, delayed, Clementine.'

'Delayed?' she repeated.

'My dear, you would never be deprived of that money.' Daryl looked horrified at the idea. 'Oh, no, you would be paid back tenfold once the deal was done.'

'You mean you want me *not* to take advantage of the codicil?'

'Well, something of the sort.'

'You mean you want me to contribute to the buying of Bruce for Amber?'

'Clementine!'

She sighed. 'I apologise, Stepfather. But no, I'm sorry, I still can't answer you. I can't, anyway, until I speak to Amber.'

'Amber loves Bruce, Clementine.' Daryl's mouth was trembling, and it looked odd on a man who appeared always unshaken.

'Amber loved a lot of things in her life, and most of them soon bored her. I wouldn't like Bruce to have that fate. I wouldn't like him wearied of, discarded.'

For a long moment Daryl looked at his step-daughter, and suddenly, intrinsically, Clemmie knew there was going to be a moment of truth.

'You're right,' he said, 'but with Amber how can one know? I don't know. Does she?'

'That's what I have to find out, find out this time for always. Can I speak to Amber when she comes?'

As though on cue, a car swept up the drive at that moment, and Clemmie's mother and half-sister alighted.

'Clementine ... Clem!' they called.

After kissing Alison's cheek, Clemmie followed her sister into their old bedroom. She sat down on her bed and she wasted no time in coming to her point. She had skirted round all this before, but this time it was for real, not for today, tomorrow, but all their years ahead.

'You've heard about the codicil to the will, Amber? Aunt Mary's will?'

'Yes—— Oh, Clemmie, can you find it in yourself to help us? Bruce has a fair amount of his own, of course, and his family's help, and Daryl will supplement it, but without Mother's inheritance, should you claim it instead, as you legally can, well—— You see I believe, *we* believe, the opposition to our offer will be extortionate. Having known Rickaby Roen' ... bitterly ... 'it would have to be that. The man is simply filthy rich. But with your support ... We'd pay you back, Clemmie. We'd promise you that.'

'I wouldn't want it back, Amber, if I did what you ask. But I would have to be sure first. I would have to be certain that you really want Bruce.'

'But I've told you,' insisted Amber.

'You've told me these things all your life, you've told me things you've needed and must have, but the next year you've forgotten them. Amber, I won't have Bruce forgotten.'

'I could never forget Bruce,' Amber said quietly. 'I love him. I don't know ... not really ... whether he loves me in return, but it still doesn't matter. You see' ... a trembling little smile ... 'I have enough love in me for both of us. Clemmie, I'd go more than half way to Bruce.'

'Then,' and Clemmie smiled fully, 'that will be enough.'

But the way things were going it was not enough for someone else. While they were having dinner Bruce came in, and he looked near-distraught.

Amber was by his side at once, and Clemmie noted the fond if slightly abstract manner in which he returned her concern.

'Trouble.' He addressed himself to Daryl Coyle.

They all waited, and Bruce told them. Roen's representative had been in touch with Osborne already, he said. He had made an offer to Osborne, an offer that his old partner, either dazzled or playing for higher stakes, had relayed at once to Bruce.

'I simply couldn't up it,' Bruce admitted.

'Clementine is here,' broke in Daryl Coyle. 'You don't seem to have noticed, Bruce,' he said shrewdly.

'Oh, yes, I did. Forgive me, Clemmie. I was shocked—still am.'

'Clementine,' inserted Daryl, 'is willing to add her mite' ... rather substantial for a mite, Clemmie thought wryly ... 'so perhaps——'

'It still wouldn't be enough,' said Bruce. 'That man must be rolling.'

'He is,' Daryl Coyle said thinly. 'He's also determined to beat you in this, or so it appears. However, I'm sure Clementine——'

'If Clemmie's kind offer was twice, three times what it is now, it still might not be enough,' Bruce admitted.

'Then perhaps,' slipped in Daryl to Clemmie, '*you* could change Roen's intentions. After all ...' But he said no more.

'You're forgetting one thing,' Clemmie reminded him, 'that is if you're suggesting what I believe you are——'

'My dear?'

'You're forgetting that I'm the Cinderella of this family—always have been, always will.'

'Ah, but at twelve o'clock you're the princess?' Daryl suggested it fancifully, humorously, but his eyes were veiled and there was a suggestion there.

'I take it you want me to win Rickaby Roen at midnight?' Clemmie said boldly.

'What a character she is!' Daryl said delightedly, indulgently. He put a banter in the words. He waited for a few moments, then:

'Clementine dear, I don't like you travelling home too late, so perhaps you'd better leave now. We'd like to keep you, of course, but we know, being our Clementine, you'll insist you don't stay.'

Clemmie did not like travelling home late, either, had not intended it, but she rose at once and said goodbye.

She did not go back to Sperry, though, and it was not a distaste of travelling over dark, unlit roads this time, it was because of Rickaby and what had been suggested to her in so many sly Daryl Coyle words. Her disgust now for her stepfather was so intense she was afraid that if she did return she might burst it all out to Rickaby, and that was the last thing she intended to do. She doubted strongly if she would ever return to Sperry, ever see Rickaby Roen again, not after that snide suggestion. She bit her lip and went firmly, after she had parked the car in the apartment lot, up the stairs, and there, leaning against her door, waiting for her, was Roen.

She made no comment, and he made none either, as she opened up and he followed her inside.

'I didn't wait after that phone call of your stepfather's to hear any explanation.' These were Rickaby's first words. 'I guessed what friend Coyle would want from you, so I instructed Rachel to tell you to go if you so wished. I then went myself. Did Coyle ask you to go across?'

'Yes.'

'Sentimental reasons?'

'If you term Amber a sentimental reason, yes.'

'Something unexpected in the will?'

'Why, yes, as a matter of fact.' She looked at him in surprise.

Rickaby looked directly back, and waited, and with a shrug Clemmie complied.

'A codicil. An afterthought, I suppose you'd call it. Aunt Mary giving me the right, if I so wished, to claim my share.'

'Of the money?' he asked.

'What else?'

'And will you?'

'No.'

'Dead sea fruit?' he queried.

'I don't understand.'

'Bruce doesn't want you any more?'

Clemmie said, 'My answer to that is that Amber wants Bruce.'

'I see. So you're going to be heroic?'

'Not at all. I don't know how Bruce feels, though I do feel sure he'll settle in time, settle wonderfully. But I'm sure now about Amber. As for me——'

'Yes?'

'Bruce is over. Past.'

'You said that before,' he commented dryly.

'This time he's as past as though it never happened at all.'

'I see,' Roen said thoughtfully again. He was being rather uncharacteristically deliberate over things. 'So you've given your share to the cause of Amber. Well done!' He gave a dry laugh and walked to the other end of the room.

'It would be,' Clemmie inserted, 'if it achieved results. But it won't be enough, will it?'

'Enough?'

'To outbid you.'

'Outbid me?' he queried.

'The Summer Heights third share.'

'So I'm in it, too, am I?'

'Of course.'

A minute went by in absolute silence, then Rickaby swung round on Clemmie.

'Look, the thing is beyond me. I've given my solicitor the figure, and that's where it ends so far as I'm concerned.'

'But it needn't be too late,' said Clemmie, 'it needn't be the end. You could cancel it.'

'The offer to Osborne was legitimate and binding. I can't back down now.'

'... Then you win.'

'Win? I don't know. Do I?' He was looking hard at her.

'What, Rickaby?'

'Clemmie, for the life of me I don't know who wins, and I don't know where I stand.'

'Of course you do. You must. You're a successful business man, and magnates always know things like that.'

'Like what?'

'Achievement.'

'I haven't achieved anything,' he said flatly.

'But you've won.'

'Yet also lost?'

'Lost?' she questioned.

'That's what I said. I told you this angle before, recall? Without his bigger stakes, his two-thirds of the promotion, Bruce won't be nearly so attractive in your stepfather's eyes.'

'My stepfather isn't contemplating marriage with Bruce, Amber is.'

'Very smart, Clemmie.' A pause. 'Then your way is clear, surely. Accept your codicil money and let that pair marry for love ... or so you say.'

'I do say, Rickaby, and with all my heart, but without the money it will only be more awkward for them. It will be harder, not easier, more involved, not more simple. It will include Mother's and Stepfather's deep disappointment, their let-down, and all because *you* wanted the majority, *you* hankered after another feather in your cap.'

'I only ever wanted one feather in my cap, Clementine. You.'

'Then——' Clemmie said, and she came deliberately across to him.

For a heady moment she thought he was going to take her, to press her to him as she never had been pressed before, not even that time she had fled from Sperry, unsure of herself, of her needs, but now ... now she knew her needs, and she waited.

The anticipation was so intoxicating she found herself even swaying. No matter, she thought a little deliriously, he would catch her to him, steady her, he would lift her in his arms, he would——

She waited.

'Goodnight, Clemmie,' Rickaby said.

'... You're leaving?'

'I have things to do. You'll be out at Sperry again in the morning?'

'I don't know. I don't think so.' Clemmie looked piteously at him.

He ignored the look. 'I'll need you. You'll be needed to wind things up. I'm leaving now, but I'll be expecting you there tomorrow, and then——'

'Then?' she asked quickly.

'Tomorrow,' was all he replied. He turned round and without another glance he left.

It was late when the apartment phone pealed. Clemmie, who was sprawled out in the big chair, who had not even found the energy to cross to her bed, picked up the receiver.

'Clementine?' It was Daryl Coyle.

'Yes.'

'I rang your place of employment.'

Ex-employment, corrected Clemmie to herself. Aloud she asked: 'Yes?'

'They said you would be there in the flat.'

'Yes?'

'Clementine, a most extraordinary thing has happened. Clementine, did you know, did you ever guess, did you ever suspect that the musical box your aunt left you was—valuable?'

'It was, and it is, *not* valuable,' said Clemmie. 'It's merely a trinket Aunt Mary picked up somewhere in her travels, something that appealed to a child's fancy, but nothing else.'

'It's *valuable*, Clementine. This purchaser——'

'Purchaser?' she echoed.

'Well, not yet, of course, I mean how could we sell without your approval—after all, dear, you were left the thing.'

'The musical box,' Clemmie murmured. She was

silent a moment. 'But how would anyone know about it?' she asked.

'These objet d'art people find out everything,' he assured her.

'But it wasn't, it was a commonplace, everyday musical box.'

'But valuable.'

'Stepfather, it's worthless,' she insisted. 'Lovable ... to me ... but worthless.'

'Worthless? Then what do you say to this offer?' Daryl named an amount that made Clemmie gasp.

'Yes, it's incredible, isn't it?' Daryl almost purred. 'Clementine, it could make a big difference to things, couldn't it?'

'Never to me. I would never sell the box, not for twice that amount. Not even for Amber.'

'Oh, we all know that you've already been over-generous, dear child, but it would be paid back, the same as the other will be paid back.'

'No,' she said firmly.

'Clementine——'

'No. Aunt Mary loved me. I think she was the only one who did love me. I know she was the only one I loved.' Clemmie stopped abruptly.

No, that was not true, and for the first time Clemmie realised it *deep down*, actually *knew* it, knew she loved Rickaby Roen, never Bruce, never anyone but Rickaby. She knew he loved her. Why, if Amber even felt half of the ecstasy of fulfilment that she was feeling in this moment, then——

'You may sell the box,' she said crisply into the phone. 'You may use the money to give to Bruce to buy out Osborne.'

'My dear, my very dear girl!'

Clemmie laid the receiver on the table. Faintly she heard her stepfather's voice going on and on in praise, and all at once she wanted to laugh. Instead she cradled the receiver back, and this time she went to bed and slept.

It was late morning when she reached Sperry, and Rachel and Gavin were out in the paddocks, Rachel doing the work that Clemmie should have been doing.

Clemmie went straight to her room, but before she put down her things she let out a disbelieving gasp. On the plain deal dressing table there was a trinket she had often wound up and listened to as a child. It was Aunt Mary's musical box, hers now ... no, that was not true, she had told Stepfather to sell it to give to Bruce to buy out Osborne.

'*I* bought it.' Rickaby must have seen her come in, for already he stood at the door. 'I reckon it must be the most expensive bit of nonsense in the world.'

'*You* bought it!' she gasped.

'For its rightful owner. You wanted it, didn't you?'

'Yes, but I also wanted Amber to have even half of what I have,' Clemmie fairly blurted. She flushed and took the box up with trembling hands.

He looked at her sharply at those words, but he did not follow them up. Not then.

'At any moment now,' he said, 'my solicitor will ring me with the sorry news that I've been outbidden for Osborne's share in the Summer Heights Estate. With the extra money' ... he waved to the box ... 'Malling will be home and dry. So you get your wish, Clemmie, yet you get your trinket at the same time. Who says you can't have your cake and eat it?'

'I still can't understand——'

'Then that makes two of us. You just said "I also

wanted Amber to have even half of what I have.''
Clemmie, what did you mean? Clemmie, I have to
know.'

'Then it's this.' Clemmie put the box down and
turned and faced Rickaby. 'I love you. I didn't mean
to—I didn't believe it when it happened. It was really
only last night when I was telling my stepfather that
Aunt Mary was the only one I'd loved, who had loved
me, that I knew——'

'Knew?' he questioned.

'Knew in all certainty, Rickaby, knew it was like
that, too, with us.'

'Yet,' he reminded her a little impatiently, impatient
with her time in explaining, 'you wanted me there last
night, didn't you, love or not. Oh, yes, Clemmie, I'm
male enough to know that. So there must have been
some knowledge then.'

Clemmie lowered her gaze. 'I did want you, but I
never associated it with love. And then—well, I just
did. I wanted you ... but I wanted your love with it.
Love, Rickaby, not just——'

'Not just this?' He took a quick step.

At last he had her in that grasp she had dreamed
about, had yearned for. She felt the fire of him, the
maleness, the mastery, the possession, but through it
all, and with it all, she felt his deep, deep caring as
well.

'Woman,' he said in her ear, 'if this was last night
and not now, it would have been a different story. I
wouldn't have walked out and left you. Clemmie, I
never will again. Do you understand that? Do you
comprehend caring as well as love? Wanting in another sense? But don't answer, darling, we're going to
keep that part of our story until tomorrow night.'

'Tomorrow night?'

'It takes more than one afternoon, you anxious baggage, to arrange a marriage.' He smiled teasingly. 'For Rachel to make a cake. She'll be sure to want to make a cake.'

'For us?' she asked.

'Well, not for Amber and Bruce. We're being married, sweet, and after that we're living happily for ever and ever. But until that time, even though I want to crush you, press you, do what I wanted to do and you wanted me to do ... yes, you did, Clemmie ... from the first moment we met, instead I'm doing this.'

He turned, and as she saw Rachel coming across the paddock with Gavin, Clemmie heard the musical box being wound. Odd, she smiled, it had never sounded like this before, not that tinkling theme of frost and ice.

For now it was warmly beautiful. It was golden harvest. Warm sands. Children's holiday voices. Trees spilling welcome shade. It was *Winter Wonderland* lost in long hot summer.

Clemmie placed the musical box to her ear, then she smiled up at Rickaby. All the days of summer, she was thinking. All the days of their life.

And there's still *more* love in

Harlequin Presents...

Do you have a favorite Harlequin author? Then here is an opportunity you must not miss!